The Bon Air Boys

The Bon Air Boys Adventures

LIGHTS

ON

WILDCAT MOUNTAIN

BY

GREG W. GOLDEN

This book is not intended to endorse or promote any of the activities by the characters contained therein. Any similarity between locations or these characters to actual places or those persons living or dead is coincidental.

The Author

Acknowledgements

My motivation in writing The Bon Air Boys series of books came from the many hours spent with our first grandchild, a wonderful preschooler named Grant. The world he is growing up in and the one of my childhood are vastly different. The influences that will pull on him are more complex than those I faced, but his options and mine are much the same. Grant can either be shaped by his world, or he can be a world-shaper!

For the reader, I hope to encourage values that are rooted in kindness, truth, loyalty, forgiveness, and a spirit of adventure in every day!

As an ordained minister, I see each sunrise as a new set of opportunities to live in God's wonderful light and love! If my outlook can be contagious, I have accomplished my mission.

My thanks in this endeavor go to my wife, Debbie; to our sons Andrew and Jonathan and their wives Christina and Emily. They all encouraged me and assisted in refining this book into what you are seeing. Our grandchildren Grant, Iris, and Ellie inspire me in their own ways daily.

Also, thank you Robert and Melinda. You both helped me greatly in this process!

About The Author

Greg Golden grew up in middle America, the youngest of three children and the only son of a pastor. Greg's love for literature was first demonstrated when at the age of ten he ran out of the forty-three Hardy Boys books available to read and he wrote one for himself.

After college, his career path took him to Mobile, Alabama, where he met and married Debbie. There they raised two sons, and those sons and wives have given them numerous grandchildren--the newest loves and diversions in their lives.

Greg is an ordained minister, and he frequently mentors those seeking encouragement and guidance who come across his path.

.

Contents

Scarcely seventy-five feet from the tire tracks and almost entirely hidden from view was a narrow entrance into the mossy surface of the hillside. The gap was wide enough to enter without touching either edge of the opening, and it was about five feet tall. A person would need to be in the perfect position and within a few yards to notice it among the thick vegetation that concealed the entrance.

"Wow! This is so cool!" Chase marveled.

"Maybe this is where the wildcats go at night!" offered Frank, partly joking but equally anxious.

"I say we check it out!" Griff urged.

Lights On Wildcat Mountain

MYSTERIOUS SIGNALS

Chapter 1

The red and white Piper J-3 Cub taxied onto the east-west runway of Burnham Field. After a short pause, it began to accelerate into the wind. The pilot pushed the throttle to the maximum, and in a few seconds, the wings created the lift needed for flight. The tail wheel rose first, and the two main wheels bore the weight of the airplane. As its speed increased, the aircraft climbed gracefully into the sky.

Griff Jenkins leaned the joystick on his remote control transmitter to the left while he eased back on the throttle. The radio-controlled Piper Cub model responded perfectly, banking gently to the north. It continued in a slow, half-circle turn until it was headed in the opposite direction.

Flying parallel to the runway, Griff leveled the wings and abruptly pulled back on the horizontal stabilizer control. With smooth precision, at the same time, he applied full power. The Piper model responded instantly, and it seemed to defy gravity as it shot almost straight up. Once it was barely a speck in the sky, Griff tugged on the joystick, and the J-3 began an aileron roll followed by a nosedive. With the skill of an ace pilot, the teenager added a few barrel rolls in the air show to the delight of his audience, neighborhood pals Chase Spencer and Frank Whidden. Griff then brought the little aircraft back home, landing it on the very place where its flight had begun.

Frank patted him on the back and exclaimed, "You are really good at that, Griff! If there were some sort of competition for radio-controlled flying, you'd win for sure!"

"Thanks! It's the next best thing to *actually* flying," Griff replied. "If I keep my grades up at school, in another year or two I want to join the Civil Air Patrol and try to earn my pilot's license."

Chase waited until Griff turned off the little engine, and he carefully picked up the model. "I'd love to shrink myself down to this size so I could ride in the cockpit! Man, what a view you could have!"

Griff laughed. "I think I'd be too nervous to fly you around in it, buddy! You never know when a gust of wind up there might take the Cub out of radio range, and I wouldn't want to have to explain that to your parents!"

Everyone chuckled at the notion of a four inch tall Chase, drifting away and out of control in the model's cockpit.

"Anybody else want to give it a try?" Griff asked.

"I'll do it!" Frank eagerly replied.

"Okay, let me top off the fuel and get it back onto the runway," Griff said, taking the model from Chase. "It's so cool that the Parks Board built this little runway for hobby people like us. It looks just like a real airport!"

Young teens Chase Spencer, Griff Jenkins, and Frank Whidden all lived within two blocks of each other in the Bon Air Village neighborhood on the east side of Lewisville. Their town of 11,000 was located along the south bank of the New Haven River. The boys' families moved into Bon Air at different times, but the three friends had known each other for most of their lives. Their birthdays fell within a span of five months, and they were inseparable as best buddies.

Griff placed the little J-3 model back onto the center stripe behind the painted number 9. The number "9" on the runway indicated a departure to the east. The orange windsock nearby confirmed a slight breeze in the area.

"All right, she's prepped for the flight. Probably at least ten minutes of fuel is loaded. Ready, Frank?" Griff asked.

Standing a dozen yards behind the model plane and with one hand firmly gripping the radio transmitter, Frank motioned a thumbs-up reply with his free hand.

Chase knelt by the plane and attached a small battery to the glow plug on the engine. Griff gave the propellor a swift spin, and the motor revved to life. Chase quickly pulled the battery connector away from the engine, and both boys stepped back. Frank manipulated the joysticks as all three boys watched the model plane gain groundspeed and then effortlessly soar into the sky of the July afternoon.

After takeoff, Frank steered the plane to the north and then guided the Piper model through a series of lazy banks, first to the left, and then to the right before circling back in the direction of the runway. At full throttle, he placed the little plane in a nearly vertical climb until the plane began to stall. He pushed on the joystick, which dropped the nose, and then he performed a beautiful recovery into a dive. Frank then directed the aircraft in a wide circle high overhead, nearly out of sight to the unaided eye.

Chase followed the action of the little plane with his binoculars. As he tracked the Piper Cub model in its maneuvers, he suddenly saw a bright glint of light--a distinct flash coming from high on the hillside. Its source seemed to be a very powerful searchlight shining from between tree branches.

"Griff, did you see that flash over there?" Chase said, pointing south into the trees near the little airstrip.

"I didn't notice. I'll look."

"There it is again!" Chase exclaimed.

The two friends fixed their gaze on the point of light coming from the upper part of Wildcat Mountain. After a minute of watching and counting the sequence of flashes, Chase spoke. *"P – M – E – N – T. It's Morse code, Griff."*

"Yeah! I see that now!" Griff reported. "It's not random, either. It's definitely a pattern, like some kind of message."

Frank had been turned away from his friends and was unaware of their discovery. Griff stepped over to him and said, "Let me have the controller for a second, please. I want to try something."

Under Griff's command, he tugged on and leaned the joysticks and aimed the Piper Cub directly at the source of the light, a quarter-mile away. As the plane reached that spot, the flashes stopped. Griff directed the Piper model to make a full circle to the east and added a second low pass directly above the area where the light source had been.

"We're going to need to land the Cub," Frank said to Griff. "The fuel won't last much longer."

Griff returned the remote unit to Frank, and after a short descent and touchdown under Frank's control, the Piper Cub model rolled to a stop.

"You did a great job, too," Chase said. "I'm impressed!"

"Thanks. But, Griff, what was that last thing you were doing flying the Cub over those trees?" Frank asked.

"We saw a reflection of the sun or some kind of really bright light in those trees," Griff said, pointing to the north slope of the mountain. "I was trying to get a reaction if anybody was in that area. It *could* have been some hikers or someone flashing a mirror, but there aren't many paths that lead way up there."

Chase added, "Yeah, if you remember, our scout troop backpacked last summer to a clearing around that spot. It was a narrow, rocky trail--very hard to climb!"

"I definitely won't forget that day. That's rough terrain. You only go up that far if you're a serious hiker," Frank replied.

While the boys were discussing the light, Frank noticed more flashes. They watched in silence, mentally noting the code letters coming from a light near the top of the mountain.

$$T - H - U - N - I - T - E$$

After a long pause and no more flashes, Frank said, "It

stopped! What do you make of all that?"

"PMENT and THUNITE. I'm clueless," Chase said. "It makes no sense at all to me."

"Okay, this is really going to bug me, guys," Griff said. "If it was just a piece of shiny foil stuck on a tree branch and blowing in the wind, I don't think we could've copied any real code letters out of it. There sure seems to be some logic in these flashes. I'm gonna jot those letters down before I forget them. Please hand me my backpack, Frank. There's a tablet and a pen in that front compartment."

After making notes of the two groups of letters, the friends discussed what they had observed. Finally, Chase said, "We should probably be heading back into town. I'll help you break down the plane, Griff, so we can pack it."

They carefully unfastened the aileron control rod and separated the fuselage and wing. Two straps of elastic secured those parts of the little Piper Cub to each other. The pieces stacked together neatly, and using lengths of lightweight rope, the boys secured the airplane sections to Griff's backpack.

The three friends boarded their bicycles and pedaled away from the airstrip. Much of the route toward the park exit was downhill, and they took care to not build up too much speed as they coasted.

Nearing the bottom of the hill, Chase was suddenly aware of the whine of a two-cycle motor. He turned his head in the direction of the sound and caught glimpses of something blue *and* fast-moving, traveling among and behind the trees. It was descending the mountain on a parallel trail, and its trajectory seemed to place it on a collision course with the boys!

"Watch out, Griff!" Chase yelled.

A heavyset man riding a powerful blue and chrome motorbike emerged without warning from a hiking trail that emptied onto the road the boys were using. The motorbike had large, knobby tires--the kind designed for off-road travel. Its rider wore sunglasses, and his shock of thick, black hair stood out wildly in the wind.

If not for Chase's alertness, Griff and the man on the motorcycle would have certainly collided. As all three boys quickly applied their brakes, the man also screeched to a stop in front of them. After a few seconds, he gunned his engine and pulled away from the boys. Chase spoke loudly in his direction, *"We're sorry!"* The motorcyclist ignored the apology, scowled over his shoulder, and shook an angry fist in the air as he sped toward Lewisville.

"Gosh that was close," Frank said. "Good job, Chase, for noticing him."

They continued another mile-and-a-half on the two-lane road through low farmland until the "Lewisville City Limit" sign came into view. As they pedaled the final quarter-mile of level ground, Griff asked, "Did any of you recognize that guy?"

"It happened pretty fast, but I didn't," replied Chase.

"I didn't either," Frank added. "The trailhead where he came out of the woods--that's the path that takes you up near the top of the mountain. I wonder if he had anything to do with that light."

"Beats me," said Griff, "but I'm going to sit down tonight and try to figure out what those Morse code letters might mean."

Arriving at their Bon Air Village neighborhood, Frank spoke. "I'd really like to hike up to the place where we saw that light coming from. There *has* to be something going on up there, and it seems pretty suspicious. Are you guys good for that, maybe sometime tomorrow?"

"Sounds fine with me, but I have another idea," Chase offered. "It's pretty crazy, but hear me out, and then tell me what you think."

....

OLD NEWS/NEW CLUES

Chapter 2

"What's your crazy idea?" Griff asked.

"Thinking about those flashing lights," Chase continued, "my cousin Donny has a remote-controlled helicopter. I haven't heard him mention using it lately, but if it still works *and* if I could borrow it, I'll bet we could attach a camera to it. We could cover more area and do it quicker than by hiking alone."

"Last Christmas I got a nice camera from my parents," Griff remarked. "It's small but has a powerful lens and some cool features. You can set a timer so it will shoot photos by itself, one picture every 5 or 10 or 15 seconds."

"I like what you two are thinking," Frank said excitedly. "That would be great to take off from the landing strip and see if we could get snapshots of anything suspicious around those trees, especially in the area where the light was flashing."

"Check with him, Chase," Griff urged. "We can use my dad's darkroom in our basement. I've helped him develop film and print photos plenty of times. It'd be easy to get to the bottom of the mystery if Donny lets us use his helicopter."

"All right, if I learn anything I'll call you guys on the walkie-talkies around 8 o'clock. And Griff, if you figure out those letters, tell us what you come up with, too," Chase said.

It was nearing suppertime, so the three friends said good-bye, parted ways and headed for their own homes.

....

Griff Jenkins was vice-president of the Math Club at Lewisville High School. He scored the best grades in Geometry of all the students in the freshman class. One of his favorite books was about the Enigma, the code machine that let the Germans communicate secretly with their troops and ships during World War II. Those coded messages kept the Allied Forces from knowing the Nazi's strategies and plans.

The government in England created a top-secret headquarters and enlisted some of the brightest minds of that time hoping to break the Enigma code. After painstaking efforts that spanned years and included the help of several European countries, the Allies successfully cracked the Enigma code. Upon doing that, they began to intercept Nazi military plans, and by using that information, it helped lead to the downfall of the German government.

After supper, Griff took a sheet of notebook paper from his binder and sat down at his family's dining room table. At the top of the page, he wrote headings above two columns: the letters "PMENT" and "THUNITE." After an hour of considering every possible word they might represent, he dropped his pencil on the table. *"We don't know what letters came before these,"* he thought to himself. *"That's what's missing. We didn't see all of the letters."*

....

Chase lifted the receiver on the wall telephone in the

Spencer's kitchen and dialed Donny's number. After several rings, he heard "Hello." The voice on the other end was of his college-aged cousin.

"Donny, this is Chase."

"Hi, Chase. How's it going?"

"It's good, thanks. I have a couple of favors to ask."

"Go for it," Donny quipped.

"Do you still have your helicopter model, the radio-controlled one?"

"Yes. Do you need it for something?"

"Well, my buddies and I were at the model aircraft runway today flying Griff's Piper Cub. We saw something on Wildcat Mountain that seemed really strange to us. We wanted to...."

Donny interrupted. "What sort of strange thing did you see?"

"Some lights were coming from the hill behind us. Actually, it was one light, but it was flashing Morse code. We wrote down the letters, and Griff is working on deciphering them. It happened twice within maybe five minutes -- two different groups of letters."

"Whoa!" Donny exclaimed. "Are you sure about that? Could it have been car headlights or something else?"

"It was bright daylight, and it was coming from within the

trees pretty high up. There are barely even *hiking trails* there. We think it was some kind of super-bright signaling light. Anyway, last Christmas Griff got a small camera that he can program to take pictures automatically. We thought maybe..."

Donny interrupted again. "So, I guess you want to attach it to my helicopter and check out that area on the mountain? Well, I don't have a problem with that. I know that you're a great radio-control pilot, but how are you going to get it up to the airfield to make that happen?"

Chase smiled to himself. "That's the other favor."

Donny laughed into the telephone. "Okay, buddy. When are we gonna do this?"

....

Frank pressed the transmit button on his base station radio microphone. "Breaker, breaker! Are you guys on your radios? Over." His receiver hissed with distant crackles of static.

"Griff is!" came the light-hearted response.

"I'm here, too," Chase said.

"Do either of you have anything to report yet?" Frank inquired.

"I'll go first," Griff said. "I'm stumped. I tried to split the letters into parts of words, and I tried to guess what letters we didn't notice that came first, but with no more than these twelve letters, I don't see how to crack this code. We need more information."

"That's tough, Griff, but I'm glad that you gave it a try. What about you, Chase? Any success?"

"Donny is good with us using his helicopter. He's going to drop it by my house in the morning. We can get Griff's camera strapped onto it, and then right after lunch, before he starts his paper route, he said he'd take us and his helicopter back up to the airstrip for the search."

"All right!!" Frank said. "We're making progress! And Griff, if you have any revelations in your sleep about those code letters, wake up and write them down, okay?"

"I'll do it," Griff chuckled. "And Chase, I'll be over after breakfast with the camera."

"Sounds good. No pressure from either of us with you figuring out the code," Chase teased, "just because you make the best math grades of everybody." He continued, "Frank, come when you can. I know you said you need to help Mr. Rigsby early, but we'll probably still be working on it whenever you arrive. 'Night guys. Over and out."

......

Leonard Rigsby lived in one of the oldest and largest homes in Lewisville. His house was an oddity in the area around Bon Air Village, and because of that, Mr. Rigsby, a widower in his mid-80s, was thought to be eccentric by the kids whose homes backed up to the expansive property that surrounded his house.

Frank began helping the elderly gentleman by doing different odd jobs and lawn mowing off-and-on over the past few years.

At 9 AM Frank bounded up the stone steps of the Rigsby house, crossed the wide front porch, and lifted the brass knocker on the front door. Through the glass panes on the sides of the door, Frank could see the frail gentleman crossing the foyer and shuffling toward him.

"Good morning, Frank. Thank you for coming by."

"I'm glad to be here, Mr. Rigsby. What project do you need me to help you with today?"

....

Donny had just left Chase's garage and was returning to his blue, two-door, Chevy coupe as Griff arrived by bicycle in the driveway.

"Hey, Griff," Donny said. "I just handed off the copter to Chase. He told me last night about the lights and the letters in Morse code. Did you do any good figuring it out?"

"I didn't. I got stuck and made no progress at all. The problem is there are probably more letters that we don't know than those we *do* know. If we could just learn a complete word or two, I think we could figure it out."

"Well, good luck with your camera. My helicopter model can lift an extra two pounds at least, so you should be fine with this experiment. I'll be back in a little while, and we can head up to the runway and put it to the test. I'm anxious to see what you guys come up with."

"Thanks, Donny. It may be nothing at all, but it's fun for us imagining that we stumbled across some mystery."

Donny had personally souped up his car, painted it to perfection, added the white, tuck and roll leather interior, and even removed the door handles. In the opinion of the three teen friends, there was no other car quite so sharp in Lewisville. Slipping behind the steering wheel and with a wave and a quick shriek of tires on pavement, Donny hollered out his open window, "I'll see you soon."

Entering the open garage door, Griff noticed that Chase had set up a table along one wall, and the helicopter model was in the middle of it.

"Here's my camera," Griff said as he placed it next to the helicopter.

Chase picked up the model and pointed to the underside. "It looks like there is a perfect spot for it on the bottom of the fuselage right between the main landing gear. We can run two elastic straps in the shape of an "X" around the camera and back through the passenger compartment. I think it'll work great there, and it won't mess up the balance."

......

"What I need you to help me with, Frank, if you don't mind, is to bring some old newspapers out of the basement and stack them on the back porch. The County Hospital has a paper drive going on now to raise money for the children's ward. I probably have enough newspapers by myself to fill half of their trailer," Mr. Rigsby said with a playful laugh. "I've had a hard time parting with *things* in the past, so down into the basement they would go. It's time to move these along and recycle them toward a good cause."

"I'm glad to help," Frank said as he descended the steps. After a minute of surveying at least a dozen years of neatly bundled and stacked editions of the Lewisville Ledger, he returned to the base of the stairs and spoke upward to Mr. Rigsby. "All of these?" Frank asked.

"As many as you have time for, Frank. I don't want to tie up too much of your morning."

"That's fine," Frank said as he put on a pair of work gloves. He began to bring the first stacks up to the covered back porch. After twenty or so trips up and down, carrying a bundle in each hand each time, Mr. Rigsby appeared on the porch with a tall glass of iced lemonade in his hand.

"Here, sit down for a few minutes and cool yourself off with this," he said while handing him the glass. He motioned Frank toward one of two wicker chairs.

"Thanks, Mr. Rigsby. I could use a break," said Frank, wiping his brow with the back of his hand. "Paper is pretty heavy when you have lots of it in bundles."

"You're right about that, Frank," Mr. Rigsby said.

Taking a sip of the cold drink, Frank glanced at the top newspaper of the last stack he'd brought up the stairs. His eyes focused on a photo of an armored truck, and then on the headlines of the Lewisville Ledger. It was an edition dating back more than ten years. Inch-tall letters dominated the front page of the newspaper, and they sparked

Frank's imagination.

"GOLD SHIPMENT HIJACKED NEAR LEWISVILLE"

There they were in black and white--five of the letters from the Morse code message, and they jumped off the page!

P-M-E-N-T!

A CLOSER LOOK

Chapter III

"Mr. Rigsby, do you remember this happening?" Frank asked, pointing to the newspaper.

"Oh, yes. It was about ten years ago, and that robbery had the attention of everyone around here for many weeks. An armored car from the east was on its way to the United States Depository to deliver gold bars. Things like that are supposed to remain top-secret, but somehow the plans concerning it leaked out."

"Did they ever catch the people who stole the shipment?" Frank inquired.

"They did not. The robbery of the armored truck happened just east of here, a few miles outside of town. Our Lewisville Sheriff's office, the FBI, and people from the Treasury Department were all over this area for weeks asking questions and looking for clues. They finally left empty-handed."

"Wow, I had no idea!" Frank exclaimed, his eyes wide with interest.

"You see, every time the Treasury Department moves gold around the country, they also put one or two decoy vehicles on the roads taking different routes to the same destination. The United States Gold Depository isn't very far from here, and a carload of very bad men took a chance on a particular armored car being the right one. They guessed correctly."

Mr. Rigsby continued. "The authorities believe that a group of them followed the *actual* shipment and then signaled ahead to their accomplices. One team of men barricaded the road *in front of* the truck, and that created a detour for vehicles traveling in the opposite direction. A second team put a different barricade *behind* the armored truck which caught it between the two roadblocks. They stole everything in that truck, and they made a clean getaway. It is still an unsolved case ten years later."

"I never knew about any of that! Right here in Lewisville, huh?" Frank marveled.

"Yes indeed!" replied Mr. Rigsby. "But I need to clarify one thing. I told you they were never caught, and that is true as far as the laws and punishment here are concerned. But, as far as God is concerned, their day to answer for the crime hasn't yet arrived."

He continued with his explanation. "You see, Frank, those criminals *think* they got away with the robbery, and for the present time they have. But, one day there will be a time of reckoning, and the things that are thought to be secret will come into the light of day. God hasn't yet pronounced judgment, but one day He will. In the Old Testament book of Numbers chapter 32 and verse 23 it says, '*Be sure your sins will find you out.*' If you or I intentionally do the wrong thing, it may not be known by others today or tomorrow, but one day that sin will be found out."

"I hadn't thought about those things like that," Frank said, rising from his chair. He handed the empty lemonade glass to his elderly neighbor. "Let me get back to work.

I think I can finish in another half-hour. We'll make this paper drive a big success with your part in it!"

......

"It looks like it's going to hold," Griff said, tugging on the camera strapped to the bottom of the model helicopter. "Whatever is still up there among the trees, we'll see it using this."

Donny stepped through the open garage door. "How's it coming? I'm back sooner than I said, but I was passing by and thought I'd check in with you guys."

"I think we have a good system, Donny," Griff said. "Come take a look."

"You want to be doubly sure, Griff. Helicopters, even model helicopters, vibrate a lot. It's just the nature of that kind of aircraft," Donny noted.

"Everything seems tight," Chase remarked, "so I think we're in good shape."

As Chase spoke, Frank arrived at his house and came through the door.

"Hey, everyone. I think I might have figured out some of the letters in the code message." Frank said as he pulled up a stool and sat down by the work table. "It's the only thing that makes sense to me right now. *P-M-E-N-T* are from *shipment*. I'm guessing that the flashes of light are from a message about a shipment! I was helping Mr. Rigsby just now, and I saw that word in the headlines of a newspaper story about an armored truck robbery of a gold shipment."

"Really?" Griff queried. "Where did that happen?"

"It was ten years ago and just east of town. I read about it in some old papers that Mr. Rigsby is getting rid of."

"Good work on those code letters, Frank!" Chase said excitedly. "If we start from there and see how other words fill in the gaps, we might make some real progress!"

Donny rose from his stool. "Well, guys, if you're finished strapping on the camera, we can get this thing up in the air. Ready to load up in my car?"

....

As they rode to the airstrip with the helicopter secured in the trunk of the car, Donny spoke. "To be honest, I'd be surprised if you're going to see very much in your photos." He wanted to prepare his young friends for any disappointment they might have after their outing.

"The camera has a strong lens," Griff said, feeling encouraged, "so if there's anything in that area that doesn't belong, I think we'll know as soon as we can develop the film and make some prints. There's enough film loaded for at least a hundred pictures."

"And if we don't get useful photos today," Chase added, "we can always hike up the trail on another day. But any clues left around by whoever was up there could be lost by a hard rain or ruined by other hikers. We can cover a whole lot of territory with your model and the camera. I'm pretty hopeful!"

Arriving at the small airstrip, Donny opened his trunk and removed the helicopter. Frank carried a canister of fuel and a battery. Griff held Donny's elaborate remote box. It had two telescopic antennas, and a wide strap that went around the operator's neck to support its weight. They all proceeded to the airfield.

Donny placed the model helicopter on the asphalt runway, directly on the center line. The windsock was fluttering from light winds in the area. Griff dropped to his knees next to the helicopter, reached under the fuselage between the landing gear, and switched on the camera. He set the timer for one photo every five seconds. The total fuel capacity allowed for a flight of ten minutes. All of the film would be used during the excursion.

Chase opened the access door on the side of the model and attached two battery wires providing the glowplug the power needed to fire the engine. Within a minute the main rotor and the tail rotor began spinning, generating a large cloud of dust. The boys shielded their eyes as Donny, from 30 feet away, applied more power. The scale model lifted into the air and hovered at eye level. After testing the tail rotor and pointing the aircraft toward the hill to the south, it rose higher and flew forward, performing and looking very much like a full-sized helicopter!

When the high-pitched whine of the motor faded in the distance, Griff leaned toward Donny and spoke while he pointed toward the hillside. "The camera is aimed almost straight down, so if you can fly above those trees, the pictures will be of whatever is underneath and between them. I feel like if there's any signaling equipment up there, we should be able to see it in the photos."

For five minutes Donny maneuvered the aircraft back and forth in a grid pattern, covering row after row of trees starting below where the first flashes were seen and then going even higher on Wildcat Mountain, above the light source. Then, for good measure, he piloted the helicopter along the ridge and followed part of the trail that led down toward the main road.

With a few minutes of fuel remaining, he guided it above the four of them where it hovered as everyone waved and smiled, the camera snapping its final shots.

After a safe landing and once Griff carefully unhooked his camera, Frank said, "I have a good feeling about this, guys. And Donny, you are amazing with that thing. It was like you've done this a hundred times!"

Donny laughed. "Try *two* hundred! You don't invest this much in a hobby and let it sit on the shelf in your basement. Hey, and I was glad to help you guys. If some great discovery actually comes out of this, and you get a big reward for catching some bad guys, I'll send you a bill for my services. Otherwise, consider it a good time among four friends."

"Either way, we owe you, Donny, and we'll make it up to you," Griff said.

....

After Donny dropped off the three boys at Griff's house, with the camera in hand, they headed through the kitchen toward the basement darkroom.

"What have you boys been up to today?" asked Barbara

Jenkins, an attractive and neatly-dressed lady who was everyone's Den Mother if they had been a Cub Scout in Lewisville.

"We've been shooting some pictures, Mom," said Griff. "You wouldn't happen to have any sodas and something to munch on, would you? We're all kinda hungry."

"I have coconut cake that I made for supper, and I think I can spare some slices of it for the three of you -- that is if you don't mind having some now and again tonight, son," she said with a smile.

"That sounds great, Mrs. Jenkins," Frank said. "I mean, um, not the part about supper, but the part about the three slices now."

Everyone laughed. "They'll be waiting for you when you're ready--three pieces and three glasses of cold milk," Griff's mom said cheerfully.

The boys descended the basement steps and closed the door behind them.

"What do we do now, Griff?" asked Frank. "I've never been in a darkroom before."

"The first part happens with no lights. You need to have total darkness when you're working with camera film," Griff explained.

He continued. "You see that rubber strip that runs around the door frame? It's there to keep any light from the out-side getting into this room. I'm going to put all the things I'll need right here in front of me because when I switch off the safelight, I'll have to work by feeling, not by seeing. You might want to lean against the wall or hold onto the counter. Trust me; it's going to get very dark in here."

....

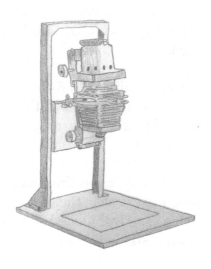

DEEP DISCOVERIES

Chapter IV

Griff turned off the red-tinted safe light and waited for everyone's eyes to adjust to the blackness of the room.

"This is *really* strange," Chase said. "I guess I don't think about the fact that even in the middle of the night in a dark bedroom there's still *some* light. In here, I can't see my hand in front of my face!"

After a few seconds, Griff continued his explanation. "So I've just rewound the film inside the camera, and now I'm opening the back of it. I've handled spools enough times in the dark to know how it feels. I'm starting to pull out the loose end of the film cartridge, and I'll thread it into the developing tank.

No one spoke as Griff skillfully transferred the film from the camera onto the spool and placed that into the light-proof tank. Then, without any warning, he switched the safe-light ON once again.

The other two boys weren't expecting that, and the newly brightened room found Chase in the middle of a yawn and Frank scratching his ear. Griff looked at both of them and laughed. "Are you two still with me?"

Griff showed his friends the different steps and bath rinses of the developing process. After several minutes he announced, "If I did this right, inside this tank should be some excellent photos. I used low-grain film that will let us enlarge anything we might find and get some great detail in our photos. We could make a print the size of a billboard out of these negatives if we needed to!"

Wearing soft, cotton gloves he removed the film from the spool. Then, using scissors, Griff cut the reel of developed film into strips of ten frames each and attached them to a clothesline stretched above the counter. He clipped a small weight to the bottom of each strip to keep the film from curling.

Griff then turned to his friends, and in his most serious-sounding voice, he said, "All right, who wants some cake?"

"You're kidding, right?" Chase asked.

"We can't stop now!" Frank exclaimed.

"Okay, okay, if you insist. Now, let's put these negatives in the photo enlarger and see what we got," Griff said. "I'm going to skip the first two strips of the film because those will be the pictures my camera took before Donny began flying over the mountain."

Inserting the third film strip and switching on the light inside the enlarger, the results of the camera's work projected onto a piece of white cardboard under the beam of the lens. The boys began to see with amazing clarity the mountainside and its trees from overhead. But what was even more important, they saw the open spaces on the ground between the trees.

"Can you zoom into this part of the picture any closer?" Frank questioned while pointing. "It looks like somebody *broke off* or *cut off* tree branches and stacked them up."

"And is that a tire track? Could we be seeing tire tracks in the dirt that far up the mountain?" Chase asked in amazement.

Griff rotated the lens and repositioned the negative strip. "Let's make a print. I think you'll be surprised at the details you're going to see once this is transferred to paper."

Griff took a few minutes to prepare the trays of developer, stop bath, and fixer.

Turning the enlarger light off, in the reddish glow of the safelight, he removed an 8 inch by 10-inch piece of photographic paper from a sealed box and placed it on the enlarger bed. From past experience, he knew how long to expose the photo paper under the light of the enlarger. Then, after moving the exposed photo paper through the three trays of liquid, he switched on the overhead room light, and everyone leaned in for a closer look.

"It's definitely a tire track," Frank confirmed. "And aren't those footprints right there?" he inquired as he pointed to several distinct and overlapping impressions in the clearing. "Griff, can you zoom in any closer on that and make another print?" he asked.

"I'd say we scored a home run here!" Chase exclaimed. "Somebody was up there very recently. It rained hard three days ago, so the tire tracks and footprints *have* to be new." He tapped on the photograph. "A signal light came from right *there* in that position. Guys, we are getting closer to figuring this out!"

After a few seconds, Frank spoke. "What do we do now? There's still so much about the message that we don't know. Maybe "*shipment*" was part of the code message, but where and when? What's being shipped? And to who?"

"I feel like we should hike up to that clearing and look around for more clues," Griff offered. "We now know for sure that somebody was there, and they went to a lot of trouble to cut an opening in the trees. Maybe they got careless and left something important behind. Anyway, I definitely would like us to *at least* make a plaster cast of the shoe print before it gets covered up or washed out."

"We can head up there this afternoon if you guys want," Frank said.

Chase joined the conversation. "Let me grab a canteen of water and some plaster powder from my garage. But first, there's the mysterious case upstairs of three uneaten slices of coconut cake."

Griff and Frank stared at their friend for a few seconds with a quizzical look, then burst out laughing. "I'll race you to the kitchen!" Griff blurted.

....

Bicycling back up the hills next to the small airstrip of Burnham Field took the friends twenty minutes. The boys turned off the park road at the hidden trailhead and walked their bikes another hundred feet up the slope near the base of Wildcat Mountain. In the covering of underbrush, they laid their bicycles over to one side of the path. They believed that no one would discover them while they were away on the high trail.

"Chase, you didn't by chance pack any extra water along with your plaster powder, did you?" Frank asked. "I'm already feeling thirsty just looking up this trail."

"I'll answer that question *if* you make it all the way up to the top," Chase teased.

"Just think back on all of those Boy Scout hikes we've done with full backpacks *and* with a pup tent strapped on," Griff said. "This'll be a piece of cake compared to those times!"

A short distance into their hike, Griff asked Frank and Chase, "Has anybody ever actually *seen* a wildcat around this place? I remember back when we did those overnight hikes, our Scout Troop leaders talked about them like they were everywhere. I always kinda figured they said those things to keep the little kids scared, and so they wouldn't wander away from the campsite after dark."

.....

The trail wound back and forth as it ascended the hillside to the high clearing, and in fifteen minutes the three hikers reached the place they had seen in the photographs. A crude handsaw had evidently been used to cut the stack of tree limbs that were visible in their pictures. The bark on the tree trunks was torn, and there were rough cuts where the limbs were missing.

Chase quickly located the shoe impressions the photos had revealed. He knelt by them and opened his backpack. Combining the plaster powder and the water, he poured the mixture into the depression on the soft ground. The plaster solution would be dry in a short time, giving the boys a replica of the sole of one right shoe.

"Let's spread out around this clearing, Griff," Frank said. "Be looking for anything that might have been dropped or left behind by whoever was up here."

"Somebody sure went to a lot of trouble to cut all of these branches and make an opening. The main thing in that direction is just the river to the north," Griff said. "I don't get the point of that."

Chase tended the drying plaster while Griff and Frank went in different directions and looked under and around the bushes and thickets beyond the clearing. After a few minutes of searching, Frank suddenly shouted. *"Guys, I found something over here! It looks like an opening into the side of the mountain!"*

Griff and Chase hurried to join him. Scarcely seventy-five feet from the tire tracks and almost entirely hidden from view was a narrow entrance into the mossy surface of the hillside. The gap was wide enough to enter without touching either side of the opening, and it was about five feet tall. A person would need to be in the perfect position and within a few yards to notice it among the thick vegetation that concealed the entrance.

"Wow! This is so cool!" Chase marveled.

"Maybe this is where the wildcats go at night!" offered Frank, partly joking but equally anxious.

"I say we check it out!" Griff urged. "Chase, you didn't happen to bring a flashlight with your plaster mold stuff, did you?"

"How long have you known me, buddy? There's one in my backpack," he replied with a grin. "I'll go grab it."

With his flashlight in hand, Chase led the way. Griff followed on Chase's heels into the damp opening of the cave. A wary Frank cautiously trailed several yards behind. "If you see any animal eyes glowing at you in the dark," Frank said nervously, "just yell, and in less than a minute you'll find me waiting for you two at the bottom of the hill!"

"Stay close to us," Chase advised, his voice echoing from inside the cave. "You'll be the *third* person to know if any wildcats live in here."

Within ten feet of the opening, the boys were able to stand completely upright. As their eyes became accustomed to the dark, Chase slowly shined his flashlight on the sides and then onto the ceiling of the cavern. Dripping trails of water coursed down the walls, collected on the floor, and flowed into the darkness beyond their view.

"Look! Footprints!" Frank exclaimed. "They go over there!" he said, pointing to another chamber twenty feet from the main entrance.

Unnoticed until that moment, the boys had been walking on damp and muddy shoe tracks--ones likely made by a person who had very recently been in the cave. Chase shined his light around the floor and confirmed that the clods of dirt led toward an opening into the second chamber room.

"There's something here on the ground!" Chase noted, leaning down to pick up a rectangle of printed cardboard. "It's a book of matches," he reported excitedly. Under the beam of his flashlight, he examined it. "It's from the Lewisville Lodge." Chase flipped the matchbook cover open. Most of the matches had already been pulled out. "Look at this!" he said. "There are some numbers written on the inside!"

The others leaned in for a better view. "That is some strange handwriting," Griff said. "See how the numbers are slanted backward instead of forward or vertical. That's pretty unusual."

"Yeah," Frank agreed. "It's what you see sometimes with left-handed people, and how they write."

"Let's check out what's in there," Griff suggested, pointing to the second room of the cave.

The entrance was larger than the one they'd first come through, and the space was much taller as well. With Frank and Griff hovering just inches behind their buddy, Chase shined his light from left to right, down, and then up.

As he illuminated the right half of the cavern, along a far wall were numerous old, wooden crates, about the size of ones used to hold soda bottles. What appeared to be lids for the crates were lying randomly nearby.

Along another wall was a metal box containing an automobile battery and a rolled-up spool of wire. The ends of the wire had metal clips like clothespins. Next to the spool was a metal base holding a slender pole that was as tall as the boys. On its top was a small version of a naval signal light! They all had the same thought. *This must be the source of the flashing light they had seen from the run-*

way!

"What do you make of all this?" Frank asked.

"I don't have any idea," Chase marveled, astonished over the discovery.

After several seconds of pondering the scene before their eyes, Griff spoke. "We have way more things to figure out now. This mystery just became *huge!*"

....

CLOSE ENCOUNTER
Chapter V

Outside the cave, the boys' minds were racing. Someone had been sending coded messages in the direction of the New Haven River with old, military-style signaling equipment. Why? And why not just use radios or telephones? Of the coded messages, the boys had seen only a handful of letters. What else had they missed?

Chase returned to the clearing and knelt by the plaster that he'd poured into the impression of a shoe. He carefully lifted the hardened cast and turned it over. Brushing away dirt and dried grass he said, "This is almost perfect. It's obviously made by a man, and you can tell from the impression approximately what size foot made this print. It's a right shoe, and the outside of the heel is worn down much more than the inside."

"That means what?" Griff asked.

"It's just how some people walk," Frank explained. "Maybe he has a limp or is a little bit bow-legged."

"This is a *wide* shoe, and long, too," Chase said as he placed the cast on the ground and positioned his size 9 1/2 sneaker next to it. "Whoever wore this shoe is a big person; I'd say he's heavy, and I'd guess he's tall, too."

Chase carefully picked up the dry, plaster cast, wrapped it in an old newspaper he'd brought, and slipped it into his backpack.

"Let's head back home, guys. We discovered more than I'd have thought we would on this trip. There's a lot now for us to think about," Frank said as he and Griff began to descend the trail together.

"I'm coming right behind you," Chase said as he stood and slipped on his backpack. Proceeding under the canopy of pine branches over the trail, he caught a glimpse of something that seemed out of place. Among the greenery was a fistful of black fibers lodged at the end of a low branch. He reached up to retrieve it. Frank and Griff continued walking ahead of him, but Chase stopped to examine the shock of synthetic hair!

He called to his buddies. "Hey, remember the guy on the trail motorcycle?" The others stopped and turned back to Chase. He held up the artificial fibers for them to see. "All of these strands are the same color as his hair. It was a *black wig*! He was wearing a *wig*!"

Chase caught up with his friends, and all three looked closely at this new discovery. "You're right Chase!" Griff exclaimed. "We almost ran into the signal light guy on his motorbike yesterday, and we didn't even know it!"

......

The grandfather clock in the Spencer house announced the hour. Most evenings at 8:00 the Bon Air Boys made a point to talk to each other from their bedrooms using their two-way radios.

As the chimes struck, Chase dropped his *Sports World*

magazine on the coffee table, left the sofa, and darted up the steps toward his bedroom. As he switched on his walkie-talkie, he heard Frank in mid-sentence calling for his buddies. "Breaker, breaker. Are your radios on? Griff? Chase?"

Chase squeezed the transmit button on the side of his walkie-talkie. "You got me!"

"Me, too!" said Griff.

Chase began the conversation. "I've been thinking about the black-haired guy on the motorcycle. I think we can assume that the light we found in the cave has been there for a while. The pole seemed pretty rusty. The battery case looked like it came out of a boat--like it was maybe a marine battery. It all seemed pretty old. He *had* to be the person that was operating it!"

"Because of that matchbook, I think we should go out to the Lewisville Lodge and snoop around," Frank said. "If the motorcycle guy isn't from around here, maybe he's staying there, and if we're lucky, we can find out his name or where he's from. Do you guys have plans for tomorrow morning?"

"Not me," said Griff, " but, I mean, we can't know for sure that he has anything to do with the signal light. The only way to connect him to that cave and the matchbook is if we find his motorcycle at the motel. It's worth the trip to find out, so I can go tomorrow. What time?"

"Let's get there early," Frank suggested. "If he's staying there, maybe we can look for his motorcycle in the parking lot before people begin checking out. How about meeting up at my place around 7:15? It's only ten minutes away on our bikes."

"The diner next to the Lodge has good food, too. Let's plan to eat breakfast there, even if we come up emptyhanded otherwise. See you early, guys. Over and out," Griff said.

"I'll be there. I'm out. 'Night all," Chase said.

....

The next morning brought thick fog and a mist that dampened the ground. That combination made seeing beyond a half-block impossible. Frank checked his wristwatch. *7:20.* He had been sitting atop his bicycle waiting for his friends in front of his garage since twelve minutes past the hour. At 7:25 he got off the bike, lowered the kickstand, and walked back into the kitchen.

"You're not giving up on them already, are you?" asked Mrs. Whidden.

"No, Mom. They'll be here."

A half-minute later a light knock on the back door ended the speculation. *"It's unlocked. Come on in,"* Frank said, turning toward the sound.

It was Chase. "Hi, Mrs. Whidden. Hi, Kate," he said.

Kate Whidden was Frank's sister. Pretty, smart, athletic, and a popular freshman at the community college nearby. Many boys in Lewisville had sought her as their girlfriend, but Kate maintained her focus on school, church activities, and making the Dean's List.

In another moment Griff arrived and pushed open the back door just after Chase closed it. "Hey, everyone. Sorry that I'm late."

Kate looked up from washing breakfast dishes at their sink. "What adventure are you guys involved in today?"

Frank spoke. "We're just following up on a little question we have after we flew Griff's plane in the city park a few days ago. We won't be gone very long."

"Be careful, boys," Mrs. Whidden encouraged, "and eat something healthy!"

"We will, Mom," Frank said as he motioned his friends toward the door and at the same time kissed his mom on her forehead.

"Bye, Kate," Chase said.

As he mounted his bicycle, Frank spoke. "So here's the plan. We're looking for a big guy on a motorcycle or at least a big guy who *has* a motorcycle, or maybe just a motorcycle for now."

"Check!" Griff replied.

"Aye aye, Cap'n," Chase quipped.

....

The fog was slowly lifting, but clouds continued to block much of the sunlight as the boys approached the Lewisville Lodge. It was a drive-up style motel--a long, one-story structure with all rooms on the ground floor. A guest could park within a few feet of their room door and enter it directly from the parking lot.

The diner adjacent to the motel lobby was a favorite eating spot for locals as well as motel guests. The smell of bacon frying filled the morning air as the boys coasted onto the property and parked their bikes near the entrance.

The parking spaces along the motel were about half-filled with cars and trucks. Scanning the length of the building Frank noted, "It doesn't look like our man is here. No motorcycles in sight."

"Let's go in and poke around a bit anyway," Griff said. "I could definitely put away one of their breakfast specials. How about you two?"

The others agreed. Within a minute a waitress led them to a booth near the entrance and placed three menus on their table.

The other half-dozen diners were engaged in soft conversations, both at the counter and among the booths and tables. A television mounted high on a wall in the far end of the room, its volume too low to hear, displayed a news program. Chase slid into one bench of the booth, and Frank followed taking the outer seat. Both of them were facing the door. Griff sat down across from them, and his view extended to the distant wall of the restaurant.

"I don't see anyone in here that fits the description of the wig guy," Griff reported as he scanned the customers. "Just some older men and some ladies with white hair."

"Well, maybe we can hang around a while and learn if

anybody checked in that might have been riding a trail bike," Chase suggested.

Their waitress returned at that moment with glasses of chilled water. "Do you boys know what you want, or do you need more time?" she asked. The three of them said they were ready, and the gum-chewing lady with an orange beehive hairdo withdrew a pencil from her apron pocket to jot down their breakfast orders.

While still at the end of their booth, she turned toward the cook at the grill and with a loud voice called for *"Three Rise-'N'-Shine specials; one over easy with hash browns and two scrambled with grits. Add extra gravy on all the biscuits."*

Once she stepped away, the friends chuckled among themselves. Frank leaned toward the center of the booth and whispered, "I guess everyone in here knows how hungry we are!"

Griff's smile was short-lived as suddenly a concerned look swept across his face. *"Don't turn around, guys,"* he said through clenched teeth. *"Our motorcycle man just stepped out of the restroom at the far end behind you. He's sitting down now at a table near the television, and he's facing in our direction."*

"Are you sure it's him?" whispered Chase. "How can you tell?"

"He's bald, he's big, he has a limp, and if you put a black wig on him, I'm one-hundred percent sure that he's the same guy!"

....

WATERBORNE SEARCH

Chapter VI

Across the cafe, less than thirty feet from them sat the man that the boys had nearly collided with when he rode his off-road motorcycle away from the hidden trailhead.

"Let's act completely normal--just three friends having breakfast," Griff said with nervousness in his voice that didn't convince Chase and Frank there was anything normal about this encounter.

"What do we do if he recognizes us?" Frank questioned.

"Yeah, if he leaves before we do, he'll have to walk right past us," Chase said.

"I tell you what," Frank began, "I'll go outside and scout a little more for the trail bike. We must have missed seeing his motorcycle *if* that really is our guy. Maybe just the two of you in a booth will seem less obvious than three of us," Frank suggested.

Frank stood, casually strolled through the diner doorway into the motel lobby, and stepped outside through the front door. He turned left and began to walk down the sidewalk past the guest rooms. Reaching the end of the building, he noticed a car coming from *behind* the motel and heading toward the highway. It was using a driveway that he hadn't noticed before. *There must be more guest rooms here than we realized*, Frank thought.

Rounding the end of the building he could see another parking lot and a dozen guest rooms that none of the boys had known were there. *Parked in front of the third room from the end was the blue and chrome trail bike they had encountered at Wildcat Mountain!*

Frank's heart beat wildly in his chest as he approached the motorcycle. He tried not to seem interested in case the owner suddenly appeared. Believing it might prove helpful to get its license plate numbers, Frank stepped off the sidewalk and into the parking lot. He made a mental note of the tag. It was from out of state: *M7G284*. Returning to the sidewalk, Frank glanced at the room number on the door closest to the trail bike. *It was the same number the boys had seen written inside the matchbook cover!*

Frank continued walking the length of the building in the direction of the motel office. Ahead of him a door from the lobby suddenly swung open and stepping onto the sidewalk was the large, bald man! He walked with a noticeable limp, and he was headed directly toward Frank!

....

Chase looked anxiously across the booth past Griff. His gaze was locked on the glass door that connected the diner to the motel lobby. "I wonder what Frank's doing."

"I'm just relieved that our man didn't seem to notice you and me," said Griff. The two friends were breathing normally again after the bald man passed them, entered the lobby, and disappeared from their view.

In another moment Frank hurried through the diner doorway and sat down in the booth. His face was pale, and he was catching his breath as he spoke. "I didn't re-alize that there was a rear exit from the lobby to another parking lot, and that there are as many rooms on the *back side* of the motel as there are on the front side."

"Really?" Chase marveled. "Our guy turned in that direction when he left. Did you see him?"

"*See him*? Frank exclaimed. He almost ran me off the sidewalk! He's huge!"

"What about the motorcycle? Was there one in the back?" Griff asked.

"Oh, yeah," he said, pulling a ballpoint pen from his jeans pocket. Frank quickly wrote down the tag number from memory on a paper napkin as his friends watched anxiously. "This may come in handy, and it's from out of state, too. Oh, and that number -- the one that was written in the matchbook that we found? It's his room number!"

The waitress arrived at that moment with a tray containing their orders. Once they thanked her, Chase said, "I'm not sure that I can still eat very much, but let me say grace over this. Bow your heads with me, guys. *Thank you, God, for this meal. Give us the wisdom to know what we should or shouldn't do next. And keep us safe. Amen.*"

"We really can't do anything about him right now. But if this guy checks out of his room, he's gone for good," Griff surmised.

"Well, Frank has the best information with that license plate number. Maybe somehow we can get his name from the front desk," Chase said.

"I don't know a lot about these things, but I don't think a motel will volunteer information to three teenagers about someone staying here. Questions like that take a search warrant, or at least you have to be older than us and look kinda official," Frank said.

The boys finished their breakfasts while exchanging thoughts and guesses. Each one gave their theory about what the lights, the cave, the wig, and the bald man meant. When their waitress returned to pick up their empty plates, she left three meal checks on their table.

"Do we pay you?" Chase asked.

"The cash register here in the diner is broken, so you'll need to pay out front."

The three boys stood and walked to the front desk. No one was in sight. Upon hearing the boys, a clerk emerged from an open door behind the counter. "How was your meal?" he asked Chase, the first of the three in line.

"It was great!" he replied while offering a pleasant smile.

The clerk rang up the meal check and announced the total. As Chase pulled his wallet from his pocket, the bell of the motel switchboard rang. The clerk looked at Chase and said, "Just a minute, please."

Turning around he put the phone handset to his ear and flipped a switch on the bank of buttons. "Lewisville Lodge. How can I help you?" A short pause followed. "Mr. Norris? Let's see…" He consulted a list next to the switchboard, "He's in room 115. I'll connect you."

The expressions on all three of the boys' faces brightened. Frank leaned forward and whispered in Griff's ear, "That's his room number, and now we have his name!"

....

The fog from earlier was gone, and the gray clouds had given way to blue skies. The boys mounted their bicycles and began to pedal home. By 9:00 they were stretched out across the sofas and chairs in Griff's den.

"Let's think about what we know and what we still don't know," Griff said. "Somebody went to a lot of trouble to send a message. I'm guessing it was to a person or people across the river using code and lights because they didn't want to use a telephone or a two-way radio. Why?"

"Because both of those can be intercepted," Frank reasoned. "Anybody can listen in on anyone's radio transmissions."

"And the police or FBI can intercept your phone calls," Chase declared, "so the message was important enough to at least *two people* to stay away from the normal ways to communicate."

"I did a little research last night in our encyclopedias," Griff said. "Using Morse code to send signals with a light, you can see it up to three miles away in bright sunlight, and five miles or more at night. So since we know the general direction the light source was pointed..."

Chase finished his thought for him. "We can draw a line on a map and get a pretty good idea where the person was who received the message--at least we can tell approximately where they were. I like how you think, buddy!"

"Do you have a map of Jeffers County?" Frank asked.

Griff was already out of his chair and walking to a book-shelf next to the fireplace. After rummaging through mag-azines and travel brochures on a low shelf, he pulled a road map from the stack and held it high in the air. "I got ya covered, Frank!" he announced.

Unfolding it on the coffee table, Frank and Chase moved in for a closer look. "There's a ruler in the kitchen drawer next to the stove," Griff said to Chase. "Would you grab it, and as you come back, there's a compass in the middle desk drawer? Bring that, too, please."

"Sure, buddy," Chase replied.

Examining the scale in one corner of the map, they noted that one inch on the map equaled one mile. Griff placed the metal point of the compass at the end of the ruler, then extended the pencil point to the three-inch mark. He then set the metal point on the image of the hobby runway at Burnham Field, and he drew an arc with the pencil to illustrate the range of a strong light during daytime.

"We have a pretty good idea which way the light was point-ed because the one we saw in the cave had a lens that made it directional. So it looks to me like whoever was receiving the coded message was somewhere around---*here!*" Griff put his index finger on a location on the north shore of the New Haven River--a lightly populated community named Clarkston. He continued. "I'm thinking the big, bald guy was sending some information to an accomplice in Clark-ston, or someplace along the river near there."

"That makes sense to me," Chase agreed.

"There's nothing much between the mountain and that three-mile point. It's mostly apple orchards and some dairy farms south of the river. There's a major hill on the far side of the river in Clarkston, so there would be a perfect view of any signal light," Frank surmised.

"Well, how do you two feel about this: I've needed to get down to our boathouse and give the *River Wind* some attention," Griff said. "How about we ride our bikes out to the marina after lunch and brush some cobwebs off the runabout? Whoever was receiving the message is an important piece of the puzzle, too. We haven't looked into *that* side of the mystery at all."

....

Griff had nearly reached the rank of Eagle Scout. He had passed the state Water Safety examination the previous summer while qualifying for the Merit Badge for Motorboating. Neither Frank or Chase had earned that distinction yet, but both of them expected to be eligible for their badges before summer's end.

Growing up in a river town, most families enjoyed the water for recreation, and the three teens were all skilled swimmers, boat handlers, and water skiers.

Arriving on their bicycles at the marina, the boys went to work in the boathouse. The brown and white runabout was suspended above the water by a motorized winch and straps. Scrubbing down the bow, hull, and stern of the fourteen-foot craft was easy in that position. Chase removed a sackful of soda bottles and candy wrappers from inside the *River Wind*. They inspected the life vests, and Frank topped off the fuel tank from cans stored nearby before they lowered the boat into the water.

The lively, little outboard motor roared to life on the first attempt, and after a cautious exit of the marina, Griff pushed the throttle forward and pointed the bow north, in the direction of the hill at Clarkston.

The New Haven River was less than a mile across when measured from the marina to their destination. Griff brought the *River Wind* down to idle speed as they reached the far shore of the river. There, he turned the boat parallel to the land. They cruised without speaking, traveling downstream a mile, and then Griff turned the motorboat upstream. They passed in front of a parking area and continued another mile. The boys searched for anything that seemed out of the ordinary. There were no houses or buildings along that part of the shore. The best possibility for a person to receive any signal messages was the scenic overlook where a half-dozen cars could pull over for a view of the river.

In their time of searching, all that they observed were a few cars passing by on the two-lane highway. Their disappointment was obvious. They would return to Lewisville empty-handed *and* out of ideas.

Griff pointed the runabout south toward their marina, and he pushed the boat's throttle ahead one-third speed. Chase and Frank relaxed in their seats.

Unnoticed by the boys, a half-mile behind them a powerful, red and black motorcycle turned into the Clarkston scenic overlook and came to a stop. The rider switched off the engine, raised the visor on his helmet, and checked the time on his watch.

....

The trio had been underway for ten minutes and were within two hundred yards of the boathouse. Frank was serving as lookout for other boats going in and out of the marina when he suddenly stood up.

"There's that light again!" Frank shouted over the hum of the motor. He pointed upward and ahead to the same place on Wildcat Mountain where they'd seen the signal flashes before.

Griff quickly pulled back on the throttle lever. The *River Wind* slowed and then quietly rocked in the blue water. As the code flashed from an opening in the trees past the farmland and beyond Burnham Field, he recited each letter aloud: *"P-L-A-N-S C-O-M-P-L-E-T-E"* There was no mistaking it!

....

AN UNEXPECTED FIND

Chapter VII

Upon their arrival at the marina, Griff carefully guided the "*River Wind*" back into the boat shelter where their journey had begun. After stopping the engine, he turned to his friends. All of the boys were visibly excited.

"I'd say whatever is about to happen it's coming soon!" Chase said enthusiastically. "The lights, the cave, the motorbike, the bald man, the code letters – we have lots of pieces to the puzzle, but we're missing the main ones."

"Yeah, and *somebody* has completed their plans," Frank said. "But *who*, and what are they talking about? What are *we* missing?"

They boarded their bikes and began cycling toward their Bon Air Village neighborhood. The shortest distance from the marina to the boys' homes took them through the town square. A block further they passed in front of the Sheriff's office.

"That's unusual," Griff commented, pointing to the two state trooper cars and a large, black vehicle with a government license plate. The three vehicles were parked outside of the Griff's dad's office. "You don't see those guys here every day."

"Well since your dad is Sheriff, I'm giving you an assignment, Griff," Frank teased. "Find out what's going on!

They might be part of our puzzle."

"Yeah, he could be sitting on the details we've been trying to figure out. See what you can learn," Chase added.

"I'll try," Griff said. "He normally doesn't talk about work once he gets home, but I'll try. In the meantime, I'm going to go back to my notes this evening and work on the first code letters we saw. Maybe I can fill in those gaps."

The three boys parted ways but confirmed their plans to talk later using their two-way radios.

....

Lee Jenkins phoned at 3:30 to say that he would have to miss eating supper with his family tonight. An unexpected, late appointment at the Sheriff's office had been added to his day.

Griff helped to clear the table following the evening meal. He and his younger sister Sally worked together to wash and dry the supper dishes. Griff put them back in the kitchen cabinets.

Alone now at the empty kitchen table, Griff randomly tapped his pencil eraser on the sheet of paper containing the incomplete code letters. He rubbed his eyes and dropped the pencil on the table. At that moment the back door opened and in stepped Sheriff Lee Jenkins.

"Hey, Dad!" said Griff. He was excited to see his father but was mentally exhausted from a solid hour of trying to break the code of the signal light letters.

Sheriff Jenkins sat his briefcase down and stepped up behind his son to rub his tense shoulders.

"Ahhhh, I needed that, Dad. Thanks! You can keep doing that for as long as you want." They both laughed.

After another moment Mr. Jenkins stopped the massage and mussed Griff's thick mop of hair. He took a cup from a hook under a cabinet near the sink and filled it from the coffee pot being warmed on the stove. "What's the problem of the evening, son?"

"There are seven letters that I'm trying to decipher. The closest I can get is "blank, blank, T, H, and then the word UNITE. There could be three or four or five letters before the T-H, but I don't know them. I've been trying to think of what those could be, and then add the word UNITE."

"That's one way to look at it, Griffin, but I think you might try another approach. What if you're dividing these words wrong? When I first looked at your paper, I saw it differently. I saw THU and NITE, like the abbreviations for *Thursday* and *night*."

Griff's expression brightened into a broad smile. He jumped up from his chair and, taking care not to spill his father's coffee, threw his arms around him. "Dad, you're a genius!! I was completely stuck and couldn't see what was obvious to you. Thank you!"

Griff grabbed his paper and pencil, sprinted out of the kitchen, and headed toward the stairs, bounding up each one to his bedroom. Lee Jenkins grinned at his son's enthusiasm and said at a volume he was sure Griff couldn't hear, "Anytime, son--anytime."

"Breaker, breaker. Are you guys on yet?"

The three boys regularly spoke at 8:00 on their walk-ie-talkies. It was 7:45, and Griff didn't expect anyone to reply.

"Roger dodger!" The voice was Chase's, the mischievous one of the trio. "What's up?"

"How about you, Frank?" asked Griff.

The radio was silent.

"I think I had a break-through with the code, Chase. My Dad was the one who figured it out. *Man, I wish Frank was here.*"

"You rang?" It was Frank's voice. "Did you say you broke the code?"

Griff continued, "Well, I was stuck for an answer, and I was seeing the letters as TH and UNITE. I got nowhere with that. But my Dad looked at my paper and saw it differently. He saw the abbreviation for THURSDAY as T-H-U, and the other letters as a short way of saying N-I-G-H-T--NITE."

Chase jumped in when Griff stopped transmitting. "So we probably have the words 'SHIPMENT' and 'THURSDAY' and 'NIGHT'."

Griff immediately added, "Plus we have the two new words 'PLANS COMPLETE' from today."

Frank returned to the conversation. "Added to all that, we have a motorcycle tire track, a big footprint, a matchbook cover from the Lewisville Lodge, and a man named Norris. It's all kind of flip-flopped, guys because we have *clues* but no crime. Now we need a crime or at *least* the possibility of one."

"I'm thinking that something important is happening someplace around here by Thursday night. Today is Tuesday, so we have just two days to figure this out," Griff said.

Chase spoke next. "One thing's been bugging me, and it's back on Wildcat Mountain in the cave. It's all those opened crates in the second chamber. We saw that signal light and the battery stored in there. We got so excited about it that we didn't bother to see what those wooden boxes were all about."

"I can't see how those things fit into these clues," Griff, said, "but if you want to head up there and check them out, I'm good with that. I'll go."

Frank spoke up. "I can't go first thing in the morning. I promised Mr. Rigsby that I'd help him for a little while around 10 o'clock. Why don't you two go ahead without me, and we can meet up after lunch. You can tell me what you learned."

Griff asked, "Are you okay with leaving at 9 o'clock, Chase?"

"Ten-four, good buddy. I'll see you at your house in the morning at 9. Over and out!"

....

The Lewisville Ledger newspaper that he held between his outstretched arms hid most of Mr. Rigsby. He was seated in a wicker chair on his porch and didn't notice Frank's arrival until he heard his sneakers reach the top step. Lowering the newspaper and peering over his wire-rimmed glasses, a smile filled the frail man's face. He greeted his young neighbor. "Hi, Frank. I hope that I didn't ruin your morning by asking you to come and help me a bit more."

"Not at all, Mr. Rigsby. I'm always glad to see you and do whatever I can to help."

"Those old newspapers that you brought up from my basement – the people from the recycling center can't arrange to come here to get them after all, so I was wondering if you could load them into my trunk. I've asked your sister to drive them to where they need to go, but I can't lift and move them. I'm afraid I would be worthless if I tried."

The kind and soft-spoken gentleman had been a friend of Frank's grandparents, Ray and Jewel Whidden, for at least fifty years. Frank's parents and the rest of his family considered Mr. Rigsby to be an adopted, third grandfather in their family.

"Sure thing. If I can have your car keys, I'll start loading them. Are the paper stacks still on the back porch?"

"Yes, son. They're right where you left them. I'm sorry to be so helpless, but this old body of mine doesn't have the strength to do what my mind still asks of it." He smiled and extended a hand holding the keys to his sedan. "It's parked in the back next to the porch."

.....

Chase and Griff were approaching the trailhead that led up to the hidden cave near the top of Wildcat Mountain.

"It gets hot mighty early these days. I could use a soda about now," Griff said.

Chase replied. "Since this is my idea, how about I buy you a root beer float at Fazelli's when we finish here? I don't want you fainting from the heat. If you did, I'd feel guilty for having this silly idea that maybe we missed a clue." His light-hearted humor was one of the traits people liked most about Chase.

Griff played along with him. "I'm not sure that just *one* root beer float will be enough. I mean, it's *really* hot this morning." He tried to sound pitiful as they placed their bikes off the trail in the same tall grass as earlier.

"If this hike up the mountain breaks our case wide open," Chase said, "I'll buy you a root beer float *and* a banana split! Deal?"

"Deal!" Griff replied.

....

Frank had transferred nearly half of the paper stacks into the cavernous trunk of Mr. Rigsby's sedan when once again he noticed the ten-year-old headline that had previously grabbed his attention. He pulled the full newspaper from under the twine that secured the pile, and he sat down on the back porch steps to read the article.

The details in the first paragraph of the story were very much like Mr. Rigsby said. A shipment that was being transported between an east coast city and the Gold Bullion Depository was in just one of three identical armored cars. Two of the vehicles were decoys and were empty. Each of them was traveling on a slightly different route, and all were headed to the Depository. They were expected at their destination within a few minutes of each other.

The team of robbers had either guessed which one was the actual shipment, or they received a tip from someone with inside information. Either way, they created a perfect situation by *isolating* and then *trapping* the real cargo between a pair of fake roadblocks. The three, stunned security personnel surrendered without any gunfire. The perpetrators disappeared with the gold, leaving no evidence behind.

Frank marveled at the genius of the method used. It seemed well-thought-out and nearly foolproof. He read further into the story and slowed down to focus on the only details the witnesses were able to offer. One of the thieves, they said, was a large man who wore a loosely-fitting ski mask to cover his face. As he was bending over the stolen cases of gold, for only a few seconds *his ski mask slipped off*. His back was toward the three occupants of the armored car at the time. They had been tied up and were seated on the ground. No one saw his face, but the witnesses agreed in their account that he was completely bald!

···········

"All right, fire up your flashlight and let's go in," Chase said as they pushed aside the thick brush that concealed the cave opening.

The two friends paused for a moment in the first chamber of the cave, once again allowing their eyes to adjust to the darkness.

Griff thought aloud, "I wonder how far this cave goes into the mountain."

"Hey, look at the signal light and the battery!" Chase exclaimed. "They're here by the entrance now, not in the second room like they were when we came before!"

"Well, that proves that we're not dreaming up those flashing lights. Someone *had* to be here yesterday when we were on the river. Let's look around and see what we might have missed the first time."

Entering the second chamber, just as they had observed a few days before, were the dozen, small wooden crates. At one time nails held the lids to the boxes, but the lids had been pried off, and now the two parts were strewn haphazardly around the floor of the cavern.

Griff squatted down and lifted one of the lids, inspecting the top and underside. He then picked up an empty case and rotated it in his hands. Brushing off years of cobwebs and mildew, his eyes widened, and he exhaled a soft whistle. Faded but still visible were the stenciled, painted letters: "*U.S.G.D.*"

"*Chase, look at this!*" Griff shouted, his voice echoing through the cavern. Chase rushed to his side and knelt next to him on the damp floor.

Both friends looked at the side of the wooden container, and then turned to face the other in the eerie shadows from their flashlights. At the same time, they quietly mouthed the words "United States Gold Depository."

PUZZLE PIECES

Chapter VIII

The importance of their discovery visibly shook them. The boys knew that they couldn't keep the cave, the flashing lights, or any of the clues to themselves any longer.

Griff spoke first. "We need to connect with Frank, and then we've gotta talk to my Dad!"

"I just hope we don't run into the trail bike man before we can get back to town," Chase said. "This is more scary than fun, now. We could be in real danger, Griff!"

They exited the cave, stopped near the entrance, and waited for their eyes to adjust to the sunlight. "I feel like no one realizes that we've been in the cave, or that we've seen the signals," Griff said. "So if we meet someone coming up the trail as we're going down, we just need to act like some kids on a hike."

"Yeah, maybe we're the only people around here, at least for now," Chase said.

No one passed them or came into view during the downhill trek. The boys' bikes were still exactly as they had left them, hidden in the tall grass. The remainder of the ride back to Lewisville was uneventful as each boy pondered the significance of the morning's revelations.

Their route took them directly to Griff's house, and they hoped Frank would be finished at Mr. Rigsby's place sooner rather than later.

....

"Mom," said Griff, "do you know if Dad is planning to come home for lunch?"

"He was," Barbara Jenkins replied, "but he called a half-hour ago to say he needed to drive over to Fairview to meet the Sheriff there. I don't look for him until suppertime, now. Do you need him for something?"

"Oh, it can wait. I just wanted to run an idea by him," Griff said.

"Well, since you're here, may I fix you two some sandwiches?"

"Actually, that would be great, Mom."

"Thank you, Mrs. Jenkins," said Chase.

The boys walked into the den and dropped into two overstuffed chairs.

"I feel like we're sitting on a keg of dynamite," Griff said in a hushed tone. "If what we've learned is true, we probably have a little more than twenty-four hours until something major is going to happen around here."

"Your dad will know what to do," Chase softly replied, trying to ease his own concerns and those of his friend. "I say we go hang out by the Sheriff's Office until he gets back into town. Then we can tell him what all we've found out just as soon as he returns from Fairview."

"I wish Frank would show up. He always has good ideas. He's not going to believe what we saw in the cave!" Griff said.

Before many minutes passed, Frank's signature knock of two raps followed by three more sounded on the back door. Both boys jumped to their feet as Mrs. Jenkins dried her hands on her apron and opened the door, inviting their buddy to come in. After a cordial hello to Griff's mom, he headed directly for the two friends who were standing in the doorway of the den. The expression on Frank's face told them that he was about to burst!

"You're not going to believe what I learned!" he exclaimed. "I was reading in the newspaper at Mr. Rigsby's...."

Griff interrupted Frank in mid-sentence, putting his finger to his own lips as a signal to stop speaking.

"Let's go up to my room," he whispered, motioning to Chase as he turned toward the staircase. From halfway up the steps, he turned to the kitchen and spoke to his mother. "Okay if Frank joins us and we eat in about ten minutes?"

"That's fine, son," she said. "I'll have it ready for you."

As the three entered his bedroom and he softly closed the door, Griff said, "Okay, tell us what you saw, and then we have some crazy news for you."

Drawing a deep breath, Frank began. "So, the robbers of the gold, when the armored car was hijacked -- they wore masks. But after the three men in the truck were tied up, they were forced to sit on the ground. The driver and the two guards didn't have blindfolds, so they could kinda watch the gang members from a distance. One of the robbers, a big man, was leaning over to pick up a container, and his ski mask fell off. None of the armored car men saw the guy's face because his back was toward them, but they told the police what they *did* see. *He didn't have a hair on his head!*" Frank concluded with a satisfied smile, and he waited for Griff and Chase to appear impressed.

"That's interesting." Chase agreed. "I guess it *could* be our bald guy, but listen to this. When we went back to the cave, the signal light had been moved from the second to the *first* chamber. That proves that *somebody* had recently been there."

Griff continued. "And the wooden crates, the ones in the second room..." he paused dramatically, then continued. "Painted on them were the letters U-S-G-D."

Frank's expression went from confused, to blank, to a big grin as he nearly shouted, "THE GOLD! Those cases came from the stolen GOLD!"

"We *can't* keep this to ourselves any longer," Chase insisted. "We need to tell everything we know to Griff's dad, but he's out of town until later today."

"I agree with you," said Frank. "Time is running out *fast*. It's already Wednesday."

"After lunch let's head into town and see if we can learn anything; maybe we can pick up on what's happening around here that we might've missed knowing about."

....

Following a hearty lunch, and after thanking Mrs. Jenkins, the boys hurried outside and mounted their bicycles. They rode toward the vicinity of the town square just as the clock in the tower above City Hall struck 1:00 PM. The Sheriff's office was a block before reaching the square, so the boys pulled into its parking lot and stopped.

"He's definitely not here," noted Griff. "Between now and tonight we *really* need to make some progress about whatever shipment might be coming to Lewisville."

"Let's leave our bikes here and walk around the square. Maybe we'll notice some out-of-towners or something unusual that'll help us figure this out," Chase suggested.

Feeling comfortable that nobody would mind, they walked their bicycles through the gate of the chain-link fence behind the Sheriff's headquarters building and leaned them against a back wall. In a few minutes, they arrived on foot at the shaded, grassy park at the center of town.

Two sidewalks crisscrossed in the tree-filled square. Benches lined the paths throughout the park. Where the walkways intersected stood a raised bandstand.

Griff, Frank, and Chase climbed the steps to the open bandstand and surveyed the businesses that faced the park on its four sides.

"I feel like it's super important that we figure all of this out," Frank said. "The Bible talks about wisdom, and if you need it, to pray and ask for it. We've been trying to unscramble all of this with just *our* minds, but we haven't asked God for any help."

"Yep," Chase agreed. "What you're talking about comes from the Bible in the book of James. Let me pray, and you two join in with me."

The three friends came together forming a huddle in the center of the bandstand. With arms over each others' shoulders and with their heads bowed, Chase prayed. *"God, you have given us good minds, and we want to use them to always do good things. Right now we are stumped, and we need wisdom. Please give us the understanding to be able to figure this mystery out and stop any evil people from succeeding with their plans. Amen."*

As they raised their heads and looked to the sidewalk below, Frank stared directly into the faces of Kate and Mr. Rigsby. Looking pleasantly surprised, he asked them, "What are you two doing here?"

"We wondered the same thing about the three of you," Kate replied. "It looks like something important is on your minds. We were just about to drop off the newspapers at the recycling trailer, and we looked over here and saw you guys climbing up on the bandstand. I thought maybe you were about to give everybody a concert or make some big announcement," she teased.

As they descended the steps to the sidewalk, the three boys greeted the elderly gentleman. Looking around the area nearby, Kate said, "I don't see your bikes anywhere. Do you guys need a ride back to the neighborhood?"

"No, we're fine," Frank assured. "We're on an information-gathering mission and just needed to check out some things in town."

"Thanks for the offer," Griff added. "We parked them at my dad's building, so we'll be fine."

"Okay, then," said Kate. "We'll be headed back to Bon Air in a little while. I'm glad we ran into you guys."

"See you later, Kate. Nice to see you, Mr. Rigsby," Chase said with a wave as the two of them walked toward the large sedan.

"All right," Griff declared, "we have some real detective work to do. Let's walk around the square and see if anything here shows up as being unusual. I don't have any idea what we're looking for, but maybe something will jump out at us."

For the next half-hour, they walked past all of the stores and offices that faced the square, and they extended their scouting to the train tracks and riverfront north of the town center. Nothing at all seemed noteworthy.

On their return to the Sheriff's office, they decided to walk down a street that was a block from where they had parked their bikes. Along the curb in front of the Lewisville Pharmacy was the metallic blue, souped-up coupe belonging to Chase's cousin. Donny was kneeling on the sidewalk beside stacks of the afternoon Lewisville Ledger. He was preparing to transfer them into his trunk and then begin his delivery route.

"Hey, Donny," Chase said as they approached him.

"Hey, guys," Donny countered as he stood up and turned to the trio. "What's going on with you three today?"

"We've been looking for anything that might answer some of the questions about those lights we saw on Wildcat Mountain," Griff explained. "A whole lot has happened since the last time we saw you."

"Man, I'd love to hear all about it. Maybe later, though, okay? I'm running behind schedule, and today I'm helping a friend who has the route north of the railroad tracks. He asked me to deliver his papers, too."

"That's fine. If we're reading the clues right, something's going to happen soon. We'll fill you in whenever it does," declared Chase.

Griff glanced into Donny's car and on the back seat sat his remote-controlled helicopter. "Looks like you still have the 'copter with you."

"Uh-huh. I just haven't bothered to take it out when I'm at home," Donny explained.

"We'll let you get back to work, but we saw you here and wanted to say hello. Catch up with you later," Chase said.

"All right. So long, guys!" Donny replied as he turned back to his newspapers.

The three friends started to walk away when Chase glanced down at the top newspaper of one stack. A photo and its caption on the front page caught his eye, and he stopped. The words in bold print sent chills through him.

....

FINAL PREPARATION

Chapter IX

The photograph in the newspaper article pictured two famous paintings. The bold words under it read *"Traveling Art Exhibit Opens Friday At Area Museum."*

"Hold up, guys," Chase declared. "Come look at this!"

He picked up the newspaper and began to read the article aloud as his friends returned to his side. *"Beginning on Friday, the Shelby Museum will feature a four-week showing of famous paintings by 19th-century Impressionist Artists. These are on loan by the Chicago Museum, and are on a year-long national tour intended to bring rare, art treasures to smaller towns across America."*

"Wow! The Shelby Museum is over in the next county, not even twenty-five miles west of here," Frank exclaimed. *"This* could be something important!"

"Does it say where the last place that art was shown? Was it around here?" Griff asked.

Chase scanned down the article and then turned the newspaper section over, following the final paragraphs to the back page. "Let's see – it's coming from the Greenville Museum and going to Shelbyville next. Guys, if the paintings are being shipped there by truck, they're probably going to come right through Lewisville! That's the shortest route!"

"The timing seems perfect," Frank agreed, stepping near Chase to read from the article. "The art showing in Greenville ended on Tuesday. Today is Wednesday. The Shelby Museum showing begins on Friday. If we're guessing right, that puts a transport truck of some sort through here on Thursday!"

"I agree with you, Frank. Giving them a little time to set things up, passing through here on Thursday makes lots of sense. Oh, we've *gotta* get to my Dad!" Griff exclaimed.

Donny was distracted from his work by the boys' excitement. "What are you guys so intense about?"

"A whole lot has happened since you helped us with the helicopter and camera," Frank acknowledged. "The photos we made there showed us that somebody had cleared an area of tree branches, and we hiked up twice to check it out for clues."

Griff chimed in. "We found a hidden cave near that clearing. You'd never see it unless you pushed the brush and branches aside. In the cave was a metal stand that held a signal light and a battery with cables to power the light. Someone had dropped a matchbook from the Lewisville Lodge..."

Chase interrupted, "...so we went *there*, and we found the big, bald guy that we'd seen on the trail bike...."

"Wait, wait – *what*? What man and what trail bike?" Donny demanded.

Frank explained. "Well, coming down from the runway on our bikes after we flew Frank's Piper Cub, we almost ran into a guy who showed up out of nowhere. He was on a motorbike on the trail that leads down the mountain. He was wearing this crazy black wig, or at least it *looked* like a wig. We didn't tell you or anyone about it because we didn't know what it all meant."

"And then we saw the same guy without the wig when we went to the Lodge to look for a motorcycle, in case the man was staying there. Sure enough, he was in the restaurant, but he didn't notice us," Griff continued. "But in the meantime, we had gone back up to the cave and saw that the signal light had been moved again. That was right after we saw more code letters in lights from the river when we were in my boat."

"You guys are either crazy, or you are onto something. So what was so interesting just now in the newspaper?"

Chase continued. "Griff's dad helped him with the code letters we saw on the first day. From those and from the second set of letters we figured out this much: It looks like there's something *very* valuable being shipped, and we believe it's coming through Lewisville today or tomorrow. We don't know exactly when, but because of this headline we now *think* it's a truck full of old and valuable paintings. They'll be coming from Greenville and will end up in the Shelby Museum west of here. The River Road is the most likely route, and it's the easiest way for a truck to travel."

"There's one more thing we didn't mention--well, actually two more things," Frank continued. "In the cave were maybe a dozen wooden crates. They were empty, but the markings painted on the lids and sides were from the United States Gold Depository. *We* believe the crates are from the armored car robbery where bars of gold were stolen when a truck was hijacked over ten years ago. Nobody ever solved that case. But the *other thing* we didn't mention is this: it seems like the big, bald guy *we* saw could be the same guy the witnesses described when that gold was taken."

Donny's jaw dropped, and for a moment he was speechless. "How could you three put all of this evidence together in only a few days when nobody else did? What does your dad say about this?" Donny asked Griff.

"He doesn't know about *any* of it, and we're trying to find him to tell him. That's why we're hanging out in town, hoping to catch him in his office. My Mom said that he got called out of town this morning, so we're staying close by until he gets back."

"Well, I'd like to know what the Sheriff says, but I've got to get these newspapers delivered. If I can help you with any of this, or if you learn more later, come find me or call me and I'll do what I can."

"We will," Chase assured him. "Thanks for the offer."

....

The boys sat down on the front steps of the police station, optimistic that any minute Sheriff Jenkins would be back from his trip. Minutes turned into sets of chimes from the City Hall clock tower that announced each quarter hour. An hour passed, then two.

"I can't hang out here with you guys much longer. I have to get home," Chase lamented. "We have some friends of my parents coming over for supper and a birthday celebration afterward."

"Yeah, I think we've waited long enough," Griff agreed. "Whenever my Dad does get home, I'll tell him what we know. Keep your radios on tonight, and I'll call you after he and I talk."

....

At 9:30 headlights swept across the front of the Jenkins house. Griff jumped up from the sofa and hurried to the back door. As he opened it, Sheriff Jenkins exited his patrol car and looked up to see his son standing on the back porch.

"Where have you been, Dad? I've been waiting to talk with you for most of the day."

"I'm sorry, son. I didn't realize you needed me. I've been doing some consulting work with Sheriff Wright over in Liberty County, and it took longer than we thought. What's on your mind?" He put his hand on Griff's shoulder. "What do you need from me?"

"Well, you're not going to believe what Chase, Frank, and I stumbled onto."

"Let's go inside. I want to hear all about it. But first I want to get some of your mom's leftovers in me. Is your mother still up?"

"Mom went upstairs a while ago, but she said she'd try to stay awake until you got home."

For the next several minutes, Griff related much of what

had happened in the past days--from the flashing lights to the boat ride; from the man with the wild, black wig, to breakfast at the Lewisville Lodge; from the headlines in a ten-year-old newspaper --to tire tracks and footprints on Wildcat Mountain.

"Here's what we think this is all about," Griff continued. "There's an exhibit of famous, old paintings coming to the Shelby Museum this weekend, and we think..."

"You think," his father interrupted, "that someone is planning to steal them. Is that it?"

"We do." He paused waiting for a positive response, then continued. "Don't you?" The silence that followed told him that the same conclusion wasn't as apparent to his Dad.

"Son, things like that rarely happen except in movies or in crime novels. I don't think you need to be concerned about any art thieves. This is Lewisville, not New York or Chicago. I believe that you saw something flashing, but I can't commit any of my men to follow or guard a truck that we don't even know is coming through here. I can't do that."

....

Griff's spirits were crushed. He sat on the edge of his bed feeling sure that he didn't want to talk with his friends at all tonight. He was afraid they'd feel he had failed to make a strong enough case for their theory. Even more than that, Griff didn't want Frank and Chase to think unfavorably about his Dad. His stomach was churning, and he only wanted to close his eyes and wake up in a new day.

He laid back on his bed and stared at the ceiling for what seemed like a half hour.

"Hey buddy, are you there?" It was the voice of Chase coming from the walkie-talkie speaker across the room.

Rising from the bed and moving to his desk chair, Griff picked up the handheld radio. "Yep. I've been tied up waiting for my Dad to get home. I told him the things we saw and did, but he didn't agree with our ideas about what's going on."

"I can hear it in your voice, Griff. Hey, don't let that get you down. We'll take another look at all of it tomorrow. If we missed the mark, well, we can hope that the bad guys don't get their opportunity, either. Frank and I talked on our radios a while ago, but when we didn't hear you at 8:00, by 9 o'clock, he said he was going to hit the sack."

"Man, I'm sorry if I blew it with what all I told my Dad."

"Don't lose sleep over it, Griff," Chase comforted. "I'm kinda' surprised the wooden cases for the gold that we found didn't impress him. That would seem like a big deal to me even if the other clues weren't that important."

Griff squeezed the transmit button as soon as Chase stopped talking. Breathlessly he exclaimed, *"I forgot to mention that!* Gosh, I didn't even bring up those cases! I told him about the signal light and how it moved between parts of the cave, and about the matchbook from the Lodge, but I completely skipped the part about the cases with letters painted on them."

"Well, maybe that'll help convince him if you can mention

those letters. I sure hope so. But, anyway, let's get together in the morning. I'll come over after breakfast, okay?"

With a renewed sense of encouragement, Griff signed off the radio conversation. He opened his bedroom door and stepped into the second-floor hallway. His parents' door was closed, and there was no hint of light coming from under it. The darkened house was silent. Telling his Dad about the best evidence the boys had would need to wait until Thursday morning.

....

SETTING THE TRAP

Chapter X

Whether it was the slamming of a neighbor's car door or the smell of bacon frying in the Jenkins' kitchen, something abruptly ended Griff's sleep. He awoke with a jolt, sat up in bed, and blinked his eyes to bring the alarm clock across the room into focus. *7:10.*

Recalling the conversation with his dad from the previous night, he jumped out of bed and pulled on some cargo shorts. After stepping into a pair of sandals, Griff ran his fingers through his hair, raced down the steps, and burst into the kitchen.

Barbara Jenkins was taking a tray of biscuits out of the oven as he came through the doorway. Seeing no one but his mother he asked, "Is Dad gone already?"

"Well, good morning to you, too!" she said leaning toward her son, kissing him on the cheek. "No, he's here. He went out to the garage for something, but he should be back in a minute."

Before Mrs. Jenkins could finish her sentence, Griff moved to the back door and reached for the knob.

His father had just closed the garage as Griff stepped onto the porch and into the morning light. Lee Jenkins looked up, surprised and pleased to see his t-shirt and cargo shorts-clad teenage son anxiously smiling down at him.

"Dad, I forgot something last night when I was telling you what Chase, Frank, and I discovered. It's probably the most important clue of all."

"What is it, Griff?" he inquired as he joined his son on the steps and walked with him into the house.

"Everything's ready," Mrs. Jenkins announced as the two closed the back door. "Orange juice, or milk, or both, Griff?"

"Just juice, Mom. Thanks."

As they took their seats at the table, he leaned toward his father and continued. "So when we went back up to Wildcat Mountain...."

"Hold that thought for just a minute, son," Mr. Jenkins interrupted. "First let me ask God for His blessing on our food and on our day."

Mrs. Jenkins stepped behind her son and gently placed her hands on his shoulders. Griff's dad touched his boy's arm as the three bowed their heads. Sheriff Jenkins prayed, *"Lord, thank you for your provisions for us and your grace to see us safely through each day. For the good rest last night, thank you. Protect and lead each of us to do the things that would please You today. Amen."*

Unfolding his napkin, Lee Jenkins asked, "All right, what is the big clue that you forgot to tell me?"

"Well, our second trip up to the cave was when we noticed that the signal light was moved from the inner room to the outer one. It was just Chase and me because Frank was helping Mr. Rigsby. What we *hadn't* paid much attention to the first time were a bunch of wooden cases spread around the floor of the second room. They were mostly over to one side. We *saw* them but didn't actually *look* at them. But when we checked them out, every one of them had some letters painted with a stencil on them: U.S.G.D." Not waiting for his dad to react, Griff blurted out, "*United States Gold Depository!*"

Sheriff Jenkins' eyes widened, and he stopped eating. He turned to Griff, looked into the distance, set his fork down, then looked at his son again. "Griff, do you realize what you just said--what you may have found? You were barely four years old when that armored truck was hijacked. How do you even *know* about it?"

Beaming with satisfaction from his Dad's response, Griff explained. "When Frank was helping Mr. Rigsby with some old newspapers in his basement, he saw the Ledger article about the truck and the stolen gold. Mr. Rigsby told him how it all happened. He said that the gold was never found and no one ever caught the robbers. The headline about the shipment helped us with some of the code letters we hadn't been able to figure out."

"Well, this could be incredibly important, son! The first thing I'm going to do when I get to my office is to send some men up to the cave to recover those wooden crates. There could still be usable fingerprints or other evidence from them that could help solve that case."

"Dad, I don't think they'll be able to find the cave on their own. It's so well hidden that *we* only found it because we were in the exact right spot searching for clues about that flashing light. Do you think I could go with your men and show them where the cave is?"

Sheriff Jenkins pushed his breakfast plate away, sipped from his coffee cup and set it down on the table before answering. "Yes, son. I think that would be good."

·········

The knock on the Jenkins's back door was from Chase. After a minute Griff's mother opened it and greeted him.

"Is Griff here?"

"I'm sorry, Chase. He and his dad left about ten minutes ago."

"Oh, okay. I had told Griff last night that I'd come over after breakfast. Do you know where they might have gone?"

Mrs. Jenkins ventured a guess. "I know that they were both anxious to get to his dad's office and then go to a cave of some sort. Griff and his dad barely ate any breakfast. Would *you* like some scrambled eggs and biscuits? I have plenty, and they're still warm."

"No ma'am, but thanks just the same," Chase said while stepping down from the porch and mounting his bike.

As he was about to exit the driveway at the street, he saw Frank approaching from a few houses away. Chase braked to a stop and waited for his friend.

"Griff's not at home," Chase reported.

"Really? Did you ever hear from him last night?" Frank

asked.

"He finally answered me on the radio after 10 o'clock. It didn't go well with his dad, and he was pretty upset about it. Then, while we were talking, he realized that he hadn't even mentioned the painted letters on the lids and crates. I guess that changed everything because he and the Sheriff are headed up to the cave right now."

"Wow! That's great news! If we've got our facts straight, today or tonight almost *has to be* when the museum truck comes through town, and we need to be ready. I guess it might end up being just you and me," Frank ventured.

"What do you think we should do? Where should we be looking?" asked Chase.

Frank explained. "I just came from Mr. Rigsby's house, and he described to me where the gold truck was stopped. It's in the only stretch of the River Road with a natural layout that would make a hijacking easy."

"It's a long shot, but it's the only chance we have," agreed Chase. "It's probably still early enough in the day that a truck wouldn't have left Greenville yet. You want to head out there now?"

"We could. I brought binoculars, some walkie-talkies, and something special in case we need it," Frank said with a grin across his face. "Crabapples and slingshots!"

"You know exactly where we're going, right?" Chase asked.

"Yep. It's about two-and-a-half miles due east of town."

········

The River Road was the northernmost boundary of Lewisville. Frank and Chase peddled from their neighborhood and rode past the Sheriff's office. They crossed the railroad tracks, continued another two blocks to River Road and turned east, traveling alongside the New Haven River. Once they passed the marina where the "River Wind" was docked, their destination, the infamous curve, was two miles ahead.

As they reached the first intersecting road, it was clear that this was an ideal place for a hijacking. The distance between the two intersecting side roads was less than a half-mile. Whatever might take place between them was hidden from both ends by a curve.

Studying the location, the boys easily imagined how the armored car would have been trapped in this very spot ten years earlier. It was a perfect setup!

"It looks like if we could get up on that bluff overlooking the road, we'd be able to stay hidden and still see whatever might happen below us," Frank observed.

"Let's try it." Chase pointed to a gap in the rusty, wire fence. "There's an opening that we can go through. We can hide our bikes in the grass and hike up the hill from that point."

Reaching the top of the bluff, the boys had a view of the River Road in both directions. In the distance to their left, the water tower for the town of Lewisville was a bump on the horizon. To the right, the concrete ribbon of the two-lane road wove in and out of view beyond the trees. Below them, they could easily see most of the curve and what they guessed would be "ground zero" for any robbery. If one was going to take place at all, they supposed it would happen in the coming several hours.

Thirty minutes went by. The passing traffic was very light, yielding only a few cars and one farm tractor pulling a wagon full of hay bales.

Passing the time with small talk, Frank spoke. "Kate was at Mr. Rigsby's house when I was there. She heard me asking him where the gold truck was hijacked, so if she was listening, she's at least *one* person who knows where we are."

Another thirty more minutes went by with only a dozen cars and a bread truck on the road beneath them.

"Do you think we've missed something?" Chase asked. "It's getting later and we haven't seen anything like a cargo truck yet."

Before Frank could answer, the distant sound of a motor-cycle engine reached their ears. Frank raised his binoculars and adjusted the focus, looking for the source of the noise. Training his view on the visible stretches of the road to the east, he shouted, "*I see something! Wait! There's a truck -- and two motorcycles behind it!*"

In several more seconds, both boys were able to see the three vehicles without the need for binoculars. Suddenly one of the motorcycles revved its engine and its front tire lifted off the ground. It sped past the truck, and in no time passed beneath the boys and slid to a stop. The rider jumped off, lowered his kickstand, and ran into the underbrush next to the road. He pulled a long, orange and white barricade across both lanes of River Road.

The museum truck was just entering the curve as the first motorcyclist completed his assignment. The truck driver, upon seeing the roadblock across his path, screeched to a stop.

Almost simultaneously, the trailing motorcycle rider went to work, quickly setting up his hidden barricade at the intersecting side road *behind* the museum truck. When his roadblock was in place, he jumped back on his motorcycle and sped to the rear of the truck.

Now, any traffic coming from the east or west was forced by the two, large obstructions to turn off River Road onto one of the intersecting side roads. No approaching drivers would suspect the fraud of those detours or the crime that was happening between them. From all appearances, the thieves were succeeding and would soon be long gone with the valuable art.

The operation had taken less than a minute. The truck with the priceless paintings was hemmed in from both sides -- caught in a simple but devastating trap! Frank and Chase, amazed and helpless, had watched it all unfold.

....

SHOWDOWN!

Chapter XI

"What was it that Frank was asking you before he left?" Kate asked Mr. Rigsby.

'We've been talking about that old incident of the armored truck carrying gold -- the one that was hijacked years ago east of town. I told him about the way the thieves managed to trap the vehicle a few miles up the River Road. I suppose you know, Kate, that no one was ever apprehended for that robbery."

"I sort of remember when that happened. I must have been about eight or nine at the time," she offered with a chuckle. "All right, are you about ready for me to take you to the market? Do you have your grocery list?"

"Yes, Kate. Thank you. I'm ready now, and it is so nice to have your help driving me around town like this," he replied.

"I'm happy to do it for you, Mr. Rigsby. It's never a problem at all," Kate said as she offered her arm to assist the elderly family friend toward the back door and into his sedan.

....

"The cave entrance is just past those trees on the right," Griff said pointing to what appeared to be a thick patch of bushes. As Sheriff Jenkins promised, two Deputies had been dispatched to accompany Griff up the trail along the face of Wildcat Mountain. They took with them large, empty duffle bags to hold the crates and lids from the Gold Depository.

From beginning to end, their mission up and down the mountain was completed in ninety minutes. By 10 o'clock Griff and the Deputies were back to the Sheriff's office.

"This is almost unbelievable, Griff," his father exclaimed. "I don't know if our lab can lift any fingerprints from these crates and lids, but if we can't, I'm sure that the F.B.I. can. Son, you and your friends have done a remarkable thing by finding these."

"Mr. Rigsby is the one who gets the credit for this," Griff answered. "None of us would've given those crates and lids a second thought if it hadn't been for his old newspapers and Frank helping him that day."

"I guess we're finished here for now. Can I have Deputy Reynolds drive you home?" Sheriff Jenkins offered.

"What I *really* need to do now is meet up with Frank and Chase. I was supposed to connect with them this morning, but we left our house and headed for the cave before I could talk with them. Thanks for the offer, Dad. Yes, I guess I'll go home and see if they stopped by or left a message for me."

As Griff and Deputy Reynolds left the Sheriff's Office and walked to the front parking lot, a car horn sounded from the street. Mr. Rigsby's large, green sedan slowed and stopped at the curb. Kate rolled down the driver's window and shouted to Griff, "I thought you'd be with Frank and

Chase. You know that they've gone up the River Road east of town, don't you?"

"No, I didn't!" Griff admitted. "When did they leave?"

"Close to two hours ago," Kate replied. "They said they were on the lookout for a moving van or a truck, or something like that."

Leonard Rigsby leaned toward Kate's open window and added, "I told Frank about the location. It's the same place where the gold was hijacked. They think something important is going to happen there today."

At that moment another car rumbled to a stop, pulling close behind Mr. Rigsby's sedan. It was Donny's shiny, blue hot rod. "What's this meeting about?" he asked with a laugh.

Griff's mind was racing. He turned to Deputy Reynolds and said, "I think I won't need a ride with you after all. I need to catch up with my buddies. Thanks for the offer."

Griff stood motionless between the two cars, and then abruptly turned to Donny. "Do you have an hour free that you can help me? I need to get to a place a couple of miles east of town – where Chase and Frank are."

"Sure! Hop in!"

Before climbing into Donny's car, Griff walked to Kate's open car window "I don't know what's about to happen, but if you could follow Donny and me, it might be helpful."

Kate looked to Mr. Rigsby, and after asking for his approval, she turned to Griff. "We'll do it, but don't lose us." Then with a mischievous smile, she added, "This car isn't quite as fast as Donny's."

Mr. Rigsby added, "Go east on River Road. The location is by the Simpson Turnoff."

....

In a few minutes, the two cars navigated the distance to the River Road and were nearing the area Mr. Rigsby described to Frank. Fifty yards in front of Donny's car, Griff and Donny saw a man wearing a dark blue jumpsuit drag an orange and white-striped barricade across the road. The detour sign on it pointed to the intersecting side road.

"That seems strange," Donny observed.

"After you make the turn like the arrow is pointing," Griff instructed, "go another couple of hundred feet and then let's pull over at the first clearing you see. I'll jump out and motion for Kate to do the same thing."

"What's going on?" Donny inquired. "Is all of this connected to the flashing lights you saw?"

"It is, and it looks like we got here in the nick of time! I hope Chase and Frank are safe," Griff added as he hurriedly opened the passenger door and stepped out. Kate and Mr. Rigsby followed them to the same clearing, and both cars were parked along the shoulder of the side road, barely clear of passing traffic.

Griff glanced into the back seat of the car. "Donny, do you

have any fuel with you for your helicopter?"

"Yep! Plenty. And the starter battery and hookup cable are in the trunk. What are you thinking?"

"Let's grab all of that and get up on that bluff above River Road. Whatever is about to happen, you and I will have a good vantage point to watch it from up there," Griff declared.

He walked back to Mr. Rigsby's sedan, its motor still idling. Frank's sister rolled down the driver's side window. "Kate, you and Mr. Rigsby, please stay here for now. I'll come back for you when we've figured all of this out."

Griff and Donny, carrying the model helicopter and supplies, sprinted up the back side of the bluff. To their great surprise, they caught a view of the other Bon Air boys, and their footsteps startled the crouching Chase and Frank.

"What in the world....? How did you....?" Chase stammered.

"Guys, it's happening now, right down there," whispered Frank as he pointed over the edge of the bluff.

Griff turned to Donny and offered an explanation. "Some art thieves are stealing a shipment of old paintings. That's what the flashing lights were all about."

Without hesitating, Donny placed the helicopter model on the ground and attached the battery. "Stand back," he instructed, "This is going to make a lot of dust."

The main and rear rotors spun to life, and Donny stood

up holding the remote control box. "Here goes!" he announced as the model lifted off. "Let's see if we can make a citizen's arrest with this thing!"

As the four of them peered over the edge of the bluff, the two thieves were in the act of tying the hands and feet of the men from the museum truck. The sudden buzzing and roar of the helicopter distracted them, and Donny took full advantage of their confusion. He directed the model into the first of many dives and low passes aimed directly at the criminals--maneuvers that only an experienced pilot would attempt.

"Grab those crabapples and the slingshots from my backpack," yelled Frank to Chase. "We've got a perfect angle from up here. They won't know what's hitting them!"

The barrage of crabapples and the persistent dives and fly-bys of the helicopter injected chaos into what the thieves *thought* would be their foolproof plan. Adding the accuracy of Frank's slingshot and supply of "ammunition," the boys and Donny kept the thieves from making headway with their departure. When they attempted to stow their motorcycles in the cargo area of the truck, the assault from above forced them to delay their exit and seek cover.

Above the whir of the helicopter and pings of the many crabapples hitting the truck, the sound of multiple sirens reached the boys' ears on the bluff. Below them and from their left, three Sheriff's cars with lights flashing pushed past the west barricade and raced into the middle of the activity. With weapons drawn, Sheriff Jenkins and his deputies quickly evaluated the situation and took control of the crime scene.

The lawmen went from stern-faced to trying to hide their laughter as they apprehended and handcuffed the would-be art thieves. The two criminals had dived under the truck to avoid the hail of flying crabapples and the relentless attacks of Donny's model helicopter.

....

Donny brought the radio-controlled model to a safe landing atop the bluff, and soon the four friends made their way back down to join the others along River Road. Mr. Rigsby and Kate had just returned in their car, and they parked next to Donny's coupe. In another moment the six of them approached Sheriff Jenkins, who was by then helping to secure the prisoners a short distance away.

"I guess I should have listened to you, son," Lee Jenkins admitted to Griff. "You boys were certainly onto something that caught everyone else by surprise."

Frank walked toward the lawmen and watched as the Deputies placed the handcuffed thieves in the backseats of their patrol cars. The face of one robber was new to him, but the second one he had seen up-close twice in the past week. It was the large, bald man! He looked at Frank through the patrol car's rear window and gave him a cold stare. It seemed to Frank that the man recognized him from the trailhead at Wildcat Mountain, or possibly from their encounter at the Lewisville Lodge. Either way, the criminal's problems were just beginning, and it would likely be a very long time before he or his accomplice would enjoy their freedoms again.

After Sheriff Jenkins and his deputies re-opened the River Road, they transported the criminals back to Lewisville for their official booking into the county jail. The occupants of the museum truck, shaken but not harmed, followed the three patrol cars to police headquarters to offer their written statements about what had taken place.

"This has been quite a day for you guys," Donny remarked, addressing Griff, Chase, and Frank. "I still have some free time until I need to load and deliver my afternoon newspapers. Could any of you guys handle a banana split or sundae from Fazelli's?"

Mr. Rigsby spoke first. "*I* sure could, and it'll be my treat! I haven't had this much excitement in a very long time!"

....

SAVORING SUCCESS

Chapter 12

The waitress at Fazelli's took the ice cream orders from Donny, Kate, Mr. Rigsby, and the three friends. While they waited for their desserts, Sheriff Jenkins entered the store from his office across the street, and he pulled up a chair to their table.

Chase turned toward him and said, "I'd like to know how you found out about the robbery, Sheriff. We thought we were on our own up on the bluff."

"I can answer that," Mr. Rigsby offered. "Once Griff and Donny started up the bluff with that helicopter, Kate and I thought that we should let the authorities know that some of the goings-on seemed suspicious to us. So, we drove ahead on the side road until we found a phone booth. We called the Sheriff and reported what we were thinking."

"What *I* want to know," Kate began, "is how you three got into the middle of this whole situation in the first place?"

"I guess you could say that we were in the wrong place at the right time," Griff reasoned. "Well, at least it was wrong as far as the thieves were concerned. A few days ago we were at Burnham Field in the park flying my Piper Cub model. In the middle of doing that, Chase saw some flashing lights in the trees on Wildcat Mountain, above us on the hillside."

"After that, we sort of just began following the clues," explained Frank. "Mr. Rigsby's newspapers and Donny's helicopter model helped a whole lot."

"When I saw your cars outside Fazelli's," Sheriff Jenkins, began, "I wanted to walk over and tell all of you what's happened since Griff and my two Deputies returned from the cave. We were able to lift some useable fingerprints from the wooden cases. It looks like we matched those old prints to a person that is known to the FBI. They belong to Bernard Norris, one of the suspects we just arrested."

"Does that mean he is one of the gold truck hijackers, too" blurted Chase, "from ten years ago?"

"Everything seems to point to that," the Sheriff ventured. "The FBI has been following his movements for a couple of months, but they lost track of him a few weeks ago. We think that using the signal light was his way of avoiding telephones or two-way radios to communicate with his accomplice. I'd say that you three were in the *right* place at the right time."

"And there's something I want to ask, guys," Sheriff Jenkins continued. "If the code message said *"Thursday nite"* what changed in your thinking for you go to River Road during the daytime?"

Chase responded, "We were pretty sure about the *"Thursday"* but never positive about the other letters. *Whenever* it happened, we were ready to stay on the bluff as long as it took, even if the truck didn't come through until after dark."

Griff added, "Once we believed we figured out *what* the shipment was, daytime made more sense to us."

Kate spoke. "You guys know from church that the wisest man who ever lived was King Solomon. In Proverbs 1 he wrote that people who aren't willing to work for their needs, but instead they take what isn't theirs, *'they ambush themselves.'* It seems that's exactly what happened. Those men planned an ambush of the truck, but it was *they* who were ambushed!"

Frank turned to Mr. Rigsby adding, "You told me the Bible teaches that everyone's wrong deeds will someday be revealed to everybody. It took ten years for Mr. Norris to be caught, but that verse sure came true for him, too."

"There's one more thing I should tell you, boys," Sheriff Jenkins began. "I can't say for certain, but there may still be a reward available if these arrests lead to the recovery of the gold from the hijacking. Don't plan on it, but it *might* happen."

Hearing that, Donny leaned forward from the far end of the table. "Hey, guys, just remember what I said to you if you three struck it rich! You don't want to forget your ol' buddy--the one who drove you up to the runway and flew your camera around the mountain strapped to my helicopter," he pleaded. *"And* the guy that helped out today!"

Chase, Frank, and Griff looked at each other, then all of them pulled the cherries from their banana splits and placed them on Donny's dessert.

"That's a down payment on your part of the reward," Chase teased. "It *might* be the only reward anybody gets."

Everyone around the table broke out in laughter. All were very thankful for the safety and successes of the day.

When The Lights Come On...

Many people today are going through life with the attitude they can do anything they want, and it doesn't matter. They act like they can say things that aren't true, bully other people, or take what doesn't belong to them. They *think* they will never have to answer for their actions. You probably know people like that. I hope that you don't do any of those things.

What they have forgotten or don't realize is that the Bible tells us something very different.

Griff, as you remember, loved solving codes. He would have enjoyed knowing Sir Isaac Newton, a 17th-century astronomer, and brilliant mathematician. Isaac Newton learned in his science studies that "every action has an equal and opposite reaction." This means that whatever we do will bring a result. The Bible says it this way: "What we sow, we will reap." If you sow (plant) an apple seed in the ground, one day you'll reap (harvest) apples from that tree.

An action that someone takes today will bring a result-- someday. A lie told will cause harm. It always does. But a kind word spoken will bring gladness. Your actions today will affect your tomorrow. Yesterday is connected to your today, and *this* day is linked to your future. *All* of your deeds, good or bad, are always seen and known by God.

(continued on the next page)

It is important that you and I always do helpful, constructive, and kind things because they please God, *and* they open up a path for blessings He wants to put into your life.

A deed done in the darkness for evil reasons will be seen by all when the correctness of God's judgment takes place. Be sure that you have nothing to hide--when HIS lights are turned on.

....

Be sure to enjoy other
Bon Air Boys Adventures
The Secret Of Hickory Hill
Whispers In The Wind
(and more!)
available from Amazon.com
Also available
as Kindle E-Books

Stay connected with
The Bon Air Boys
and the author by visiting
BonAirBoys.com
There you will find latest
information about
upcoming books and products.

Made in the USA
Monee, IL
02 December 2021

82872326R00069